the REBOUND

New York Times & *USA Today* Bestselling Author

KENDALL RYAN

The Rebound
Copyright © 2021 Kendall Ryan

Copy Editing by Pam Berehulke
Cover Design and Formatting by Uplifting Author
Services
Photo by Sara Eirew Photographer

About the Book

My coach hates me, and our team captain now watches my every move, so that's super fun.

Which is why I'm trying something new—being a good guy. It might not be what I'm known for, but I'll try anything once.

The part of this that's not an act? Helping out my new neighbor Kinley. She's beautiful, funny and newly single. (*Score!*)

There's just one problem. She's also the team captain's sister.

There are rules about this kind of thing. But rules were made to be broken.

1

SAINT

When Coach Wilder asks you to stick around after practice with his permanent stink-eye cranked up to full power, you stick around.

Even if there's a hot girl waiting for you at a high-end bar just a short drive away. Even if her open-minded best friend is there too, and you've all made arrangements to party back at your place after a couple of drinks. *Ménage à trois* pending.

No, you forget all that, shower fast, change, and get your ass to your coach's office in all of ten minutes.

With a couple of minutes to spare, I'm towel-drying my hair when my phone buzzes. My cracked screen shows I have three messages.

thanks for calling ahead and opening your tab babe.

u really are a saint :)

cece and i just ordered shots. hurryyyy

Grinning, I take a low-angle photo of my glistening abs and attach it to my response.

just showering for you babes ;) be there soon

"Are you seriously sexting right now?"

I look up to find our starting center, Alex Braun, doing what he does best. Judging me.

Stashing my phone in my pocket, I resist the urge to roll my eyes. "When demand is high, I gotta supply. Oh shit, that rhymes. Think I should get it tattooed on my ass? You're the expert of ass tattoos, aren't you?"

Alex scowls at me, but a grin widens across his face before he can help it.

The poor bastard lost a bet with me last year and now has a heart-eyed emoji on his left ass cheek. I'd say he definitely got the better end of the deal, seeing how he'll be marrying the woman that

I bet he'd fall for. He gets the gorgeous Aspen on his arm for the rest of his life, and I get to make fun of him for the rest of mine. It's a win-win situation.

"Such a player," is all he can manage to say back, shoving my shoulder not hard enough to hurt, but hard enough to make me lose my balance.

Why do people call me a player? So what if I want to enjoy my life and have fun . . . how is that playing games? Sex positivity is a thing, and I enjoy the hell of it.

I pull a Boston Titans T-shirt on over my head before heading out of the locker room and down the hall toward Coach Wilder's office. My back's been bugging me lately, and I'm sure he's noticed it affecting my posture on the ice. I'm not sure how I pulled it, but it could have something to do with my most recent blackout adventure at the club . . . which, I'll admit, wasn't my finest moment.

It's not like I make it a habit of letting my social life interfere with my work. I'd even argue that my work-life balance is pretty damn healthy. After all, hockey isn't a sport for athletes who can't commit to excellence. The game is brutal and the rules are strict—so strict, in fact, that I can't be bothered to follow any other rules in life. I give my one hundred percent to the team, and the rest of it? You guessed it. Fast cars, eager women, and enough cash in my pocket to bribe the bouncer. Gotta let loose somehow, right?

I knock on Coach's cracked-open door, interrupting a hushed conversation inside. "Whoa, the party is in here," I say jokingly, misreading the room.

No one laughs. Tough crowd doesn't even begin to cover it. Coach is flanked on both sides by our team captain, Walker Reeves, and the Boston Titans' owner, Eden Wynn.

Coach and Reeves look up with blank expressions, but Eden narrows her eyes at me. She's never really liked me, seeing as I'm tight with her ex, Ass-Tattoo Alex. The two of them are all good now, but she's still not my biggest fan. Probably blames me for the team's poor public image, now that Alex has renounced his bad-boy ways in favor of being a total bore.

"I'll leave you three to it," she says, giving Coach Wilder a pointed look before breezing by me without so much as a greeting.

I must be in some pretty deep shit.

A smirk twitches at the corner of my mouth. Who am I kidding? I love a little trouble.

"Take a seat, Saint." Coach's voice is stern, but

no more than it usually is. The man needs a vacation, and I'm not the first to say it.

On my way to the chair, I spot a small stack of paper sitting in the printer tray. From the obnoxious header logo of the one on top, I can already tell what this conversation is gonna be about—I've hit my bad-behavior quota this month, and it's time to lay low. At least until next month.

"You can probably guess what this is about," Coach says with a weary sigh. The man's not much older than any of us, but the stress of the job is already painting strands of silver in his hair. Poor guy. He's the youngest coach in the league, so he's got a lot to prove.

"I haven't been keeping up with the tabloids," I say with a sly grin, scratching my chin. "What'd I do this time?"

Reeves *really* doesn't like that response. He picks up the stack of papers and tosses them on the desk in front of me. I flip through the headlines, waiting for them to spark memories.

Spotted Shirtless at the Sinclair: Price St. James Goes Wild

Saint or Sinner? Exotic Dancer Tells All About Night Out with Boston Titans Defenseman

That last one rings a bell, and I have some bruising on my back to prove it. Honestly, I'm a little impressed with myself.

I chew on my smile, hiding it behind an amused frown. "Pretty cool that they're all different."

Reeves glares at me, shaking his head in disbelief. "No, Saint. Not cool. Not cool at all."

Looks like Coach isn't the only one in need of a little rest and relaxation. Reeves disappears to Mexico for about a month every summer to surf, and I hope for all of our sakes he's getting on a plane as soon as this meeting ends and our summer officially begins.

"I mean, it's the off-season. Can't you cut me some slack?"

"This," Reeves says, waving the papers, "is what happens when we 'cut you some slack.' So, no. We can't. This shit has to stop."

"I know, I know. I'll cool it, okay?"

"You're gonna do a whole lot more than just cool it." Reeves chuckles humorlessly. "Consider yourself on probation."

"Probation? From what, living?"

Reeves rolls his eyes and throws his hands in the air.

Okay, I'm a little pissed now. If Reeves wants a fight, I'm more than happy to give him one. The guy has had it out for me since day one. We're polar opposites. If life were an amusement park, I'd be the guy who heads straight for the biggest, steepest ride as soon as I walk through the gates, fast pass in hand. Reeves? I doubt he'd pull the stick out of his ass long enough to even enjoy the teacups.

Coach Wilder stares me down. "We're tired of the stories, Saint. Every day it's something new. We've got donors calling us, complaining. Your actions don't only affect you—they affect the whole team. But you'll be dealt the worst of it. Sooner or later, you're gonna find yourself strapped with a lawsuit, or worse? Injured. Because you can't seem to just get drunk anymore. You have to get reckless too. It's too much."

I sink back into the chair, wincing when my back twinges.

Maybe he has a point. Maybe I've been partying too hard lately. Maybe it's because all my friends are getting hitched, and every engagement party I have to attend makes me want to crawl out of my skin. Maybe I'm panicking.

My expression turns serious. "Okay, I'll get it under control. No more headlines."

Reeves cuts in. "Seriously, Saint. One more and you're suspended."

When I shoot a wide-eyed look at Coach, he nods solemnly. *Dammit.*

Coach pinches the bridge of his nose and lets out a long sigh. "This is serious, Saint. Keep a low profile this summer. No trouble for the team. Got it?"

"Fine," I force out between gritted teeth. "Is there anything else?"

"That's it." Coach sighs again. "See you tomorrow."

Tomorrow is our dressing room clean-out and an optional workout. I didn't really plan on coming in, but I guess I am now.

Abruptly, I stand, letting the chair screech against the linoleum floor before I make my quick exit. I don't even bother closing the door behind me.

My gut burns at the memory of Reeves's smug expression, his self-righteous indignation. What a fucking asshole. On top of all this shit, now I gotta force myself to play nice with the captain, who hates me now more than ever? *Great*.

When I round the corner, I spot Alex and Tate heading toward the exit, and call out, "Hold up."

• • •

Thirty minutes later, Alex, Tate, and I are crowded together in a booth at the nearest bar. The beer in front of me glistens like heavenly nectar, but I leave it untouched. I've lost my taste for it, still reeling from the meeting.

"They want me to live like a monk." I clench my fists under the table. I haven't been this pissed in . . . I don't even know how long. Adding insult to injury is that I'm missing out on the company of *two* women tonight.

Alex shakes his head. "That's rough, man." He's been on the other side of that desk more times than me. He gets it.

"Maybe it'll be good for you," Tate says. They are words I *really* don't want to hear.

The rookie is a good guy, *too* good for my liking. Ever since he returned from a trip to Colorado with a brand-new wife in tow, he doesn't even come out much with us anymore.

I scoff at him, dipping my fingers in my beer and flicking them in his direction. "Some of us have a pulse, rookie."

"Dude."

Alex rolls his eyes, tossing Tate a napkin. "Chill, Saint. He's right. You could use a break. No girls. No parties. Just hockey. It can only do good things for your career. That's what you want, right?"

Spoken like a true reformed playboy. Alex's career definitely hit its stride when he realigned his priorities, I'll give him that. It *should* be what I want too.

But me? A life without the freedom to do whatever I want, whenever I want, would be disastrous for my sanity. Every man has his outlet, and mine is being with people, *new* people, in exciting scenarios. Extrovert—that's what my mom would call me. That reminds me, I need to call her. I missed our chat last Sunday.

Sometimes my personality gets me in some pretty crazy spots. But that's part of the fun, right?

"Anyone in there?"

Alex lightly smacks the back of my head, and it's like my thoughts tumble right out of my skull and onto the table so I can see them clearly. It's a bad situation, and the guys are just trying to help me make the most of it. I can't fault them for that.

"Yeah, yeah, yeah. You're right," I mutter, begrudgingly agreeing. What else is there to do? I've gotta play nice with the captain now.

"So, are you really going on the straight and narrow?" Tate shoots me a mocking look. "Should we be making bets for how fast you fail?"

Alex peers at me over the lip of his glass of beer, then shakes his head at Tate. "Nah, no bets. Just support."

Gratitude swells in my chest. This asshole. He's a better man than me, that's for certain.

I treat him to a grin. "Thanks, man."

"Anytime." He smiles back.

The guys finish their beers and do the whole act like they're not excited to go home to their adoring women, saying some "ball and chain" nonsense. I see right through that horseshit. Alex adores his fiancée, Aspen, and Tate and Summer are like a couple of heart-eyed emojis whenever they see each other.

I can't help but wonder if I'll ever get suckered into a relationship someday. Will it be a gradual discovery, like with Alex and Aspen? Or a whirl-wind of emotions, like Tate and Summer? Both scenarios sound pretty damn unlikely for me. Especially since that's the last thing I'm looking for right now.

I step outside to find my car, pulling my phone out of my pocket to check the time. My phone buzzes with about a thousand missed messages and phone calls.

Fuck. Looks like I forgot to text my hot date and her open-minded best friend, Cece, about the change of plans.

The messages are a mix of confusion, anger, and eventually just a slew of drunk, blurry photos to prove what a good time they're having without me. I don't even want to know how much they put on my tab. I guess I'll find out when the bar bills my ass.

After sending an apology text and calling the bar to put a cap on my tab, I pocket my phone and take a deep, sobering breath.

All things considered, taking a break from the fast lane to enjoy a gentle cruise might not be the worst thing I've ever done. I've been on the merry-go-round of life long enough to make anyone else dizzy. Time to stop and enjoy the view.

Let's hope I don't lose my mind in the meantime.

2

KINLEY

My feet hurt. My back hurts. And I have to pee *all the time*. Oh, and my freaking gums have started to bleed whenever I brush my teeth. Do I have some sort of degenerative disease? Am I dying a slow, excruciating death?

Nope. I'm just really, *really* pregnant.

Whoever said pregnancy is a blessing must have either never been pregnant or had some sort of magical Zen baby growing inside them. My little guy? When he's not practicing his high kicks, he's taking a long snooze directly on top of my sciatic nerve. Who can blame him? It's probably so nice and warm in there. But my precious little angel might be trying to kill me.

Okay, that's an exaggeration. I'm happy to be

having a kid. Happier than I thought I would be when those faint pink lines first appeared on my pregnancy test.

I remember letting out a breath I didn't realize I'd been holding during those excruciating four minutes of waiting. I was sitting on the bathroom floor of my then-boyfriend's apartment, who I'd just started to see seriously a month prior. Staring at the chipped tile, I debated what to do. He and I were in a brand-new relationship . . . could we really raise a baby together? I still wasn't even sure where our relationship was going.

Nowhere, apparently.

Because when I told him, he responded as I'd expected. He flat-out panicked about how a baby would affect *his* life. Then his brain short-circuited and he could only utter monotone one-word responses. I decided to give him time to process the information I'd barely processed myself. One of us had to be an adult.

The next morning, he went to stay with a friend and left me a note that basically said, *Good-bye, good luck, and leave the key under the mat.*

Awesome.

I still don't really know what came over me, but after that, I was determined to be the best mom possible. So I moved halfway across the country to be close to the only man I can truly count on—my brother, Walker.

We haven't been very close in a long time and have drifted apart over the years. But he came through when no one else did. When I finally called him to share the news, he immediately asked what he could do to help me. I swear I almost burst into tears.

Fast forward two months, and I'm moving into the condo directly next to his—that he paid for in full. Too generous? Absolutely. But buying another condo didn't even make a dent in his bank account. My brother is a professional athlete with plenty to spare.

My career as a digital marketer hasn't been quite as lucrative. And it wasn't like I was about to pass up on the opportunity to no longer be homeless, bouncing from one friend's couch to another. My self-preservation instincts are much stronger than my pride.

Plus, the chance at a fresh start, away from all my mistakes? Sign me up.

I did draw the line at one point. After fully purchasing and furnishing the condo, Walker suggested he cancel his annual surf trip to Mexico to be here for me. It took some convincing on my part, but we eventually settled on these terms: he'd still go on his well-deserved vacation, but only for two weeks instead of four. I agreed to call him if I needed anything . . . *anything*, he emphasized. I'm still surprised he didn't make me sign a contract.

I've been on my own for the majority of this pregnancy, and I know I can take care of the two of us by myself. Having my brother helicopter around me has been undeniably helpful, but an independent woman like myself can only take so much micromanaging.

I'm a freelancer, a profession I slid haphazardly into after one too many arguments with my raging asshole of a boss. I'm good at being my own boss, reveling in the freedom to create my own schedule and work on projects that I actually care about. I answer to no one but myself, and let me tell you, that's been a game changer for my stress levels.

Now the primary stressor in my life is having this dang baby. That, and carrying this enormous package down the hallway to my condo. My joints scream in protest as I do my best to lift with my legs, taking breaks along the way.

"Little guy, I'm about to rip open this box and start carrying these books one by one," I mumble, running a soothing hand over my belly. I like talking to him like he's already a full person. Makes me feel a little less alone, you know?

I groan, struggling with the box. I asked my friend to mail me my library of books that she's been graciously housing for the last few months while I got my life in order. I just didn't think she'd send them all in one box.

Holy back pain, Batman.

"Need a hand?"

A man's voice calls from over my shoulder, and I suddenly realize what I must look like from behind . . . leaning heavily against the wall, sweating through my pregnancy romper, my hair piled up on my head and looking like a perfect home for baby birds.

Wait until I turn around, buddy. You have no idea what you've signed up for.

I turn around, pregnant belly in full, magnificent view. "I would *love* a hand."

But he doesn't flinch at all when he catches sight of me. The voice belongs to a man in his late twenties, with a shock of dark blond hair that's messy on top but tapers down into a close crop on the sides. He jogs the rest of the distance and lifts the box with the ease of an experienced weight lifter.

Why, hello.

"Where to?" he asks.

"End of the hall, second to last door on the right."

"After you."

I lead the way, talking to him while trying to catch my breath. "Thanks so much. I know that thing weighs a ton and a half."

"Who's mailing you bricks?"

"Books, actually." I laugh, immediately appreciating his sense of humor. "Someone clearly didn't think it all the way through when mailing the heaviest package in existence to the single pregnant lady."

His gaze makes a quick perusal of my figure, but his expression remains impassive. "I always thought pregnancy gave you superhuman powers. Even more so when you're single."

I chuckle, shaking my head as I unlock the door. "Not in my experience."

Ignoring everything I've been taught, I open the door wide for a stranger, somehow knowing I can trust him not to be a serial killer. Inside, he sets the box gently on the living room floor. He winces a little as he straightens, twisting his torso from side to side until I hear a loud crack.

"Back issues," he says with a crooked smile.

"Oh my God, are you pregnant too?" I tease.

His blue eyes dance on mine. "Not quite so lucky. I just overexerted myself."

"Working out?" The question slips out of my mouth before I have the common sense to shut up.

Did I just ask a stranger if he works out? I mean, he obviously does. His baby-blue T-shirt and gray joggers stretch comfortably over lean, tough muscles. His forearms have those pronounced veins that trail down to his large hands, each of which are neatly manicured. The man takes care of himself.

"You got me." He winks at me, and I can't help but smile.

Who is this guy?

"What's your name? I'm Kinley. I just moved to Boston this week."

"I'm Saint. I live down the hall to the left. Welcome to the building."

I reach out and shake his hand. His grip is firm, but not crushing like some assholes in the corporate world. Like, we get it, hearty handshakes make for good impressions. Don't break my fingers.

"You're really kind for a complete stranger."

"Happy to help. Is there anything else I can carry in?"

I blink at him, a laugh hovering on my lips. "Really?"

He nods. "Really. I've got nothing better to do."

"Nothing better to do than help your pregnant neighbor carry her packages upstairs?"

"Seems like."

I shrug, considering letting him off the hook. I mean, I don't want to take advantage of his kindness, but then common sense gets the better of me. I'm seven months pregnant, and I don't know why I thought I could manage all this on my own.

Hesitantly, I tell him about the awkward package shaped like a disassembled desk down in the mail room and ask if he'll bring it up to me. It's the same desk I've had since I graduated from college with nothing but a measly marketing degree to prove my worth. I bought the desk as my first real purchase—for me and *only* me. It's small and worn, but it means the world to me.

Saint agrees. After retreating downstairs, he returns with the box in a matter of five minutes. When he offers to set up the desk for me too, I get suspicious.

"What's in it for you?" I ask, my eyes comically narrowed.

It's not like I don't trust the guy . . . he's been nothing but helpful. He hasn't said anything creepy or tried to hit on me. But then again, since I got pregnant, I seem to have a sign taped to my belly that says **DAMAGED GOODS—RUN AWAY** in big red letters. Men don't traditionally flirt with a woman who has a baby on the way. Which is more than fine, since I'm not in the market for a man anyway.

"Not a thing." He flashes a brilliant grin that throws me a bit.

Every woman in this building must have a crush on this dude. I sneak a peek at his hands again. No wedding ring.

Interesting.

But his unexpected offer for help is exactly what I needed, if I'm being honest. I'm still adjusting to my new figure. I always imagined I'd be one of those cute pregnant people, maybe with the luxury of an expanded chest size, which is something I've never had.

The reality has been strikingly different.

For starters, I tire more easily. And don't even get me started on my body. My boobs are still small. Actually, most of me is the same size—except for my belly, which looks like I swallowed a cantaloupe. It sticks out proudly, proclaiming my condition to anyone in the vicinity.

There's no hiding my condition, not that I would want to. The belly has also come with a few unexpected perks, like people happily waving me up to the front of the line at the post office, and extra packets of ketchup from the fast-food cashier with my fries. The right amount of ketchup is very important.

Saint is still flashing that crooked smile at me, so it takes me a second to respond.

"I'm grateful for the help and want to do something for you. Hey, I've been craving Thai food, so I'm going to put in an order. I'll get you whatever you want. And don't say you don't want anything, because then I'll just order you something random and force you to eat it."

He raises his hands in surrender. "Pad Thai. Tofu, medium spicy. I'm a simple guy."

"I appreciate simple."

The food should arrive in thirty minutes, plenty of time for Saint to finish setting up my desk and for me to prop up my sore feet for a while. The little guy in my belly kicks *hard*, and I gasp.

Concerned, Saint looks up from his work. "You good?"

"Oh yeah. Channing Tatum here is just reminding me that he's got some killer dance moves."

Saint chuckles, and I can't help but notice the adorable dimple in his left cheek. You'd have to be blind not to notice the guy is seriously attractive.

When the doorbell buzzes a short time later, I look wearily toward the door. Ten feet never looked more like ten miles.

"I'll get it." Saint jumps up and is at the door in no time at all, speaking in a low voice to the delivery girl.

In one minute flat, I have a warm container of gooey, delicious noodles sitting in front of me. Starving, I dig in, and when the flavors hit my tongue, I make a sound so involuntarily filthy that I can't help but blush.

"Sorry, it's just so good."

"Don't apologize." Leaning against the kitchen island, Saint makes a whole show of slurping up his first bite, his eyes rolling back in his head and filthy sounds of his own filling the whole room. When he finally recovers, he smirks at me. "Gotta get your jollies wherever you can."

I cover my mouth with my hand, chewing around a boisterous laugh. Saint is totally on the same wavelength as me with a sense of humor that I find most men to be lacking. "I'd offer you something to drink, but I haven't had the chance to really stock the fridge."

A look of concern crosses his features. "Do you have what you need?"

Thinking about it, I tilt my head. My brother left me with a couple of gift cards to some grocery stores that deliver. I've been wanting to explore the neighborhood more, though.

"I should probably try to get to the store soon."

"Do you have a car?"

I shake my head. "I'll have to research where to go."

"Want me to take you?" Saint asks it so nonchalantly, like we've known each other our whole lives, not less than an hour. Like it's as easy as breathing.

Is it crazy to say yes? Am I really that desperate for a helping hand? For a little companionship? Still, I can't accept his offer. We just met, and he's already done me two favors.

"No, that's okay." I take another bite but notice he's still watching me.

Saint raises his brows at me. "I'm free tomorrow, so I could show you around. Since you're new to the area and all."

"No, I couldn't. Thank you, though."

He meets my eyes with a kind expression. "I really don't have any other plans. It would give me something to do."

Sensing that he's serious, that maybe he'd just be sitting around bored and alone, I give in. "It would be nice to have someone show me around a bit."

"Cool. Does tomorrow at two work for you?"

"Uh, yeah." Anytime would work for me.

"It's a date. I'll take you wherever you need to go."

Smiling, I cock my head to the side. "I'm not completely helpless, you know."

Saint gives me that crooked grin again. *Wow*. My insides do a little happy dance. "Helpless? Never said you were. You're doing me the favor here. It's rare I have something productive to do with my time. I was gonna throw myself out the window if I had to spend another moment flipping channels."

I chuckle again. "If you say so."

We spend a few minutes eating our noodles and making polite conversation, mostly about the groceries and houseware supplies that I need. For the first time in a long time, I'm starting to feel like everything is going to be okay. Maybe things will work out for me here.

If an experience with a total stranger can be this pleasant—*fun*, even—then maybe my life in Boston won't be so bad after all.

3

SAINT

If you had told me two days ago that I'd be comparing prices for prenatal gummies in the vitamin aisle, I'd have told the bartender to cut you off. Yet here I am, and stranger yet? It feels completely normal.

Kinley stands next to me, our shopping cart filled to the brim with houseware items and a few essential groceries. She peeks around my shoulder with a frown. "Woo, look at those prices."

"Not great," I say before tossing both kinds of gummies in the cart. At twenty dollars a bottle, they're more than even I was expecting, and I take a lot of pricey supplements. "They're on me."

"No way," she says, swatting my arm playfully.

"Ouch." I cry out in pretend pain.

A man looking at protein powder peers down the aisle at us.

"Oh my God, stop." Kinley giggles, gently rubbing my arm where she smacked me. "I didn't even hit you that hard."

"It's those hormones," I say. "You're hulking out."

Kinley scrunches up her nose in an adorable way, lifting her fists. "Then you'd better not mess with me." Her smile is absolutely contagious.

"Copy that."

We've been wandering around the store for more than an hour without a real plan in mind. Normally, I'm the kind of guy who finds shopping boring. I have a *get in, get what I need, get the hell out* kind of mentality. But with Kinley, shopping isn't boring at all. For starters, I keep finding ways to make her laugh. And if the number of times she's snorted between giggles is any indicator, she's having a pretty good time too.

Coach and Reeves think I'm some reckless partier who needs to clean up his image. I'm not saying they're wrong. I'm just saying, what could be more wholesome than taking your single, pregnant neighbor out shopping for life essentials? Prenatal vitamins, no less. I'm half waiting for some boy scout's badge of honor to appear on my sleeve.

Although, my motivations for helping her have nothing to do with wanting to clean up my image. I'm enjoying myself and not overthinking things beyond that.

When we wander past the shoes selection, I snag a pair of plush slippers off the shelf and offer them to Kinley. She looks up at me with a grateful smile, and damn, if that doesn't fill me with a warm sensation.

If I'm being honest with myself, this errand run isn't just some do-gooder chore I'm checking off a karmic to-do list. Helping a neighbor in need is the right thing to do, of course, but I'm actually having a lot of fun while I'm doing it.

As we pass the freezer aisles, an idea comes to me that I immediately share. "I vote we grab ice cream after this."

"Ooh. Seconded."

"Do we have a third?" I look down to where her stomach sticks out, as if I'm waiting for the baby's input.

Kinley laughs again before rubbing her belly with one slender hand. "My personal magic eight ball says, 'all signs point to yes.'"

I chuckle. "Then it's settled."

When we're ready to pay and leave, I find myself checking out more than just our shopping haul, stealing a few glances at Kinley while we load the items onto the conveyor belt.

She's pretty, no question. Gorgeous, really, with her long dark hair flecked with gold and her wide hazel eyes. Kinley hasn't told me much about how she ended up pregnant and single, but from what I've gathered, the guy she was dating didn't care to stick around when he found out the news.

Which makes me wonder . . . what kind of man in his right mind would leave a woman like Kinley? She's smart as hell, with a wit that's got me stepping up my usual smack talk because the girl can handle anything. Not to mention her killer sense of humor. She makes me laugh and keeps me on my toes.

While Kinley is distracted, searching through her bottomless pit of a purse for her wallet, I sneak the opportunity to whip out my card and hand it to the cashier. He nods apathetically and runs it without a word.

When Kinley finally looks up, wallet in hand, I'm already shoving the receipt in my pocket. Her eyes are wide and an awed smile sits crooked on her face. "You didn't . . ."

"I know. It wasn't my place. But I did," I say with an innocent shrug. I don't know her well enough to know if she's actually mad, or just plotting out a way to pay me back.

She shakes her head at me in disbelief, but the sparkle in her eyes is enough to tell me that she's not mad. "You really are a *saint*, aren't you?"

I've heard the line a million times, but for some reason, when Kinley says it, it feels brand new. "So they tell me."

Fifteen minutes later, I'm parking the car next to my favorite ice cream shop. It's a little corner store with a classic red awning and a line of families spilling out the front door. I open the car door, feeling the summer heat roll off the asphalt in waves. It's late in the afternoon at this point, and the sun is unavoidable with minimal shade options. I'm not about to let Kinley stand in this heat for God knows how long, so I leave the car running.

"It's hot as balls out here, so you hang tight. Air-conditioning is here on the dash, or you can just roll your window down for a breeze."

"Thank you. I'm burning up." She sighs, leaning her seat back.

I catch a glimpse of her glistening cleavage as she adjusts her top, then look away before I can get any ideas. "I'll get you a bottle of water too, if you like."

"That would be amazing."

"What flavor of ice cream do you want?"

She taps one finger to her chin, contemplating. "Hmm. Surprise me."

"Surprise you?" Not what I expected . . . but I like a challenge.

"Yeah." She cocks her head to the side, daring me. Kinley's only known me for two days, and the woman can already tell how much I love a good challenge.

"You got it. And for the little guy?" I nod, glancing at her stomach.

She chuckles, patting her belly gently. "I think we'll share."

The line moves quickly, and in under ten minutes, I'm back with a little cardboard cup of limoncello for me and an ice-cold bottle of water and a cup of chocolate peanut butter for her. She squirms happily in her seat at the sight of the thick swirls of peanut butter and white chocolate chips.

"Yesss, you read my mind. Thank you," she sings before wrapping her lips around a heaping spoonful. Her eyes flutter closed, and she hums in happiness.

Mission accomplished.

We eat our ice cream at the curb in comfortable silence. When we're finished, I hop out of the car and shove the empty cups in the closest trash can.

As I get back in the car, Kinley stifles a yawn. "Wow, I'm wiped. How are you doing?"

"I'm golden. Let's get you home."

The car ride back to the complex isn't very long, but Kinley still dozes off with her head resting lightly against the window.

A tender feeling seizes my heart.

I've never had someone fall asleep while I was driving, except that one time I drove the rookie back to his place when he was blackout drunk. This feels different somehow, more meaningful. Kinley trusts me completely to get her home safely.

I glance at her belly as it rises and falls with her serene breathing. A strange, foreign thought occurs to me.

For the first time ever, I've got a baby on board.

How about that?

When I pull into the parking garage at our complex, Kinley is still sound asleep. I don't want to wake her, but we don't know each other well enough for me to carry her upstairs. I quietly unload the shopping bags and bring them inside before coming back for Kinley. When I open the passenger side door, she jolts awake.

"Hey, it's okay. We're home," I say softly. I consider placing a comforting hand on her knee, but Kinley blinks a few times and recovers before I can decide whether it's a good idea or not.

"Oh, I fell asleep, didn't I? Sorry. These days I'm always on the brink of a nap."

"It's no problem. Come on, let's get you inside."

I offer her a hand, and Kinley accepts it. Her palm is soft as silk, and her grip light and pleasant. A shiver climbs up my arm and spreads across my chest.

Just going to ignore that sensation for now.

Since her feet are swollen from walking around all day, Kinley lets me help her up the stairs. Once we're in her condo, she gestures to the couch with her half-empty water bottle.

"There. Just leave me there to die."

I chuckle, following her lead to the couch and steadying her as she lowers herself with a huff. Once I'm sure she's comfortable, I look her in the eye and deadpan, "Rest in peace."

Kinley lets out a low laugh from deep in her chest, sinking into the cushions. "Peace, huh? What would you say at my funeral?"

I take a moment to contemplate this while I'm stacking pillows beneath her ankles. "She had a great sense of humor and very swollen feet."

"Deep," she says, her eyebrows hitching. She takes a gulp from the water bottle before stifling another yawn. "Thanks for your help today. You're really the best neighbor I've ever had. Or maybe I'm the worst neighbor you've ever had."

I shrug. "Like I said, nothing better to do."

It's true. If I weren't here, I would just be sitting alone at my own place, probably playing video games. Maybe getting tempted to get into trouble. At that thought, I glance around, deciding I might as well continue to make myself useful.

While Kinley dozes, I wander around her condo, putting away the new purchases one by one. New air fresheners in the bathroom. Paper towels and cleaning supplies under the kitchen sink. Two kinds of prenatal vitamins on the kitchen island. Four bags of frozen broccoli in the freezer.

Huh. I guess she really likes broccoli.

Laundry detergent and fabric softener in the cupboard above the washer and dryer. A small succulent in the living room on the window ledge, where it will get plenty of sun. The new pair of plush slippers outside of her bedroom door.

While I organize whatever I can, I walk past the second bedroom door, which is cracked open a couple of inches. Inside, the walls are painted a soft beige just like the rest of the condo, and boxes of diapers are piled on the floor.

This must be the nursery.

I almost peek my head in for a better look, but think better of it. I'd rather have Kinley show it to me herself. Besides, there's not much to see. It doesn't look like she's done much with the space yet.

I'm tempted to start helping her unpack the rest of those moving boxes too, but that feels a little more personal than unpacking the shopping bags we filled together just a couple of hours ago. I glance at my watch, seeing almost dinnertime, and wonder if I have enough time to go back to my place and whip something up for her while she's still asleep.

"What time is it?"

I turn to see Kinley standing up from the couch, rubbing the sleep from her eyes. She smiles at me, refreshed from the short but much-needed rest.

"Almost dinnertime."

"Oh man, I must have slept for a while. I'm a terrible host."

"You were tired. I hope you don't mind that I went ahead and put away as much as I could."

She looks around, taking in the view of a tidier living space. "Are you kidding? That's so nice of you. I'm . . . whew." She blinks back some tears and swallows. "I'm getting emotional. Will you let me make you some dinner as a thank-you? I really can't be indebted to you like this. It's too much."

"Kinley, it's really okay—"

"Please? I love cooking. It wouldn't be a hassle for me. Plus, I'm starving. You'd be doing me a favor." She uses my own words from last night against me with a knowing smile.

I rub the stubble along my jaw, uncertain if accepting a favor from a pregnant woman will somehow undo all the good karma I've earned today.

You know what? Screw karma. I like spending time with Kinley. And if she wants to make me dinner, then why the hell not?

"Sure, I'm down."

"Awesome." She sighs in relief. Looking toward the kitchen, she chews on her lower lip. "I don't actually have a lot to work with here. My grocery order doesn't come until tomorrow . . . Do you like broccoli?"

I nod. "I do like broccoli, but I have a better idea. Why don't we move this party to my place?"

It's a phrase I've said in many bars to many women, and I only realize the implication once the words are hanging in the air between us like a swarm of red flags. The last thing I want is for Kinley to think I'm some creep.

Backpedaling, I lift my hands in the air. "I, uh, went grocery shopping a couple days ago, so you'll have more ingredients to work with than just broccoli. That is, if you're okay with that scenario?"

Smooth save, Saint. But if Kinley suspects anything, she certainly isn't giving any indication.

Smiling innocently at me, she shrugs. "I think that would be best."

Well, damn. Guess I'm taking a pregnant lady home with me.

That's a first.

I guess the new Saint is having lots of firsts lately.

4

KINLEY

Saint's place is nice. Like, *really* nice. And I'm not just saying that because I've been stepping around half-unpacked moving boxes for the past week. No, his condo looks like a page torn out of a minimalist interior design magazine.

Everything is monochromatic and clean, satisfying the undiagnosed OCD in me immediately. And since the layout of our condos is almost identical, I'd be lying if I didn't admit that I'm actively taking mental notes on how to arrange my own place. His living room holds a large navy sectional that faces the windows, and his round dining table fits perfectly into the nook off the kitchen. Three upholstered bar stools are lined up at the island.

"Shoes off?" I ask, not wanting to track any dirt

onto his sparkling floors.

"Whatever's more comfortable for you." But he kicks his shoes off, so I follow suit.

"Did you design all of this?" I gesture to the space.

Saint grins and scratches the back of his head. "Yes and no. Don't laugh, but my mom is an interior designer. She personally hates this style, but I stole a few ideas from her over the years and adapted them to better suit me and my preferences."

"It's beautiful. You must have a good job to afford all of this."

He nods a little reluctantly. "Yeah, well, I've been doing the same grind for the past four years and it's paid off. How about you? What do you do to afford all that broccoli?"

I chuckle. "Don't act like you didn't pay for my broccoli too. I do just fine. I'm a freelance digital marketer with a focus on brand creation."

He raises his eyebrows. "Sounds fancy."

"It's good enough for now," I say before looking down at my belly. "Once this guy is out and about, I'm going to have to decrease my hours in order to take care of him. No more twelve-hour days on the phone with clients."

"My schedule is really flexible during the summer," Saint says, and I almost think he's bragging until he says, "so if you need any help running errands or whatever, I'm your man."

I'm your man. The phrase would make me blush if it weren't so innocently delivered. His kindness has been unexpected, but also very appreciated.

"I appreciate that more than you know." I'm about to ask him what it is that he does for a living that gives him that kind of flexibility, but he waves me into the kitchen.

Just like the rest of his condo, every appliance is in pristine condition. The espresso machine in the corner catches my eye, and all other thoughts dissolve into a massive craving for coffee.

Saint follows my line of sight. "You want some coffee?"

"No, I'm off caffeine right now. Hence all the naps."

"I could make decaf."

Shaking my head, I say, "I'd better not. It'll just confuse my body."

"Ah, well, once the little guy is here, you can come over and make yourself some espresso anytime."

I narrow my eyes at his back as he opens the fridge. I thought his name was fitting before, but now I'm pretty sure he's an actual angel on earth.

"All right, we've got all sorts of produce . . . zucchini, tomatoes, potatoes, fresh garlic, arugula—"

"Geez, you eat really healthy foods."

"Don't be fooled. There are at least ten frozen pizzas in here." He chuckles, tapping his knuckles against the freezer door. "I went to the farmers' market recently and left with enough produce to feed a small army."

"There's a farmers' market nearby?"

"Yeah, every Saturday from eight in the morning until sundown. If you're around next weekend, I could take you."

"You know me. I've got no plans."

Even as I say *you know me*, I think how silly that must sound to him. We've only just met. But I really do feel like Saint and I have become fast friends. Faster friends than any other friends I've had, at least. It's nice to just *click* with someone so quickly, even if it is the last thing I expected.

I clear my throat. "If you have any bread, I make a mean vegetarian panini."

"I have some sliced multigrain and some ciabatta."

"I can work with that. Throw me the ciabatta."

It's a quick and easy recipe that I learned during my brief stint as a vegetarian back in college. Simmer some onions and tomatoes in a pan with a little sugar until it reaches a jammy consistency, season and sauté some zucchini, and then slap it all on bread slathered with garlic mayo. Panini-press the whole sandwich, if you have one, which of course Saint does.

When it's all done, I plate the sandwiches for us while Saint looks on, impressed.

We sit down at the small dining table strategically positioned by the window overlooking the courtyard. The sunset casts a warm glow across the whole room, making my companion's dark eyelashes create shadows against his high cheekbones. I haven't had the chance to make food for another person for over half a year now, so watching Saint's eyes light up when he takes his first bite is all kinds of fulfilling.

"This is really fucking good," he says, mid-chew.

"I'm glad you like it." I beam at him, taking a bite of my own.

Yep, that hits the spot.

Over dinner, we talk more about summer in Boston, what there is to do, what there is to see. It's not long before our plates are empty and our appetites satisfied.

When I stand up to clean up the kitchen, my feet scream in protest. Saint must notice my wince, because he quickly takes the plates from my hands and urges me to sit back down.

"I've got it. You just relax."

I sigh, feeling a little helpless in my condition. I used to be able to do everything by myself. It's humbling to have my body remind me to slow down like this.

After dragging my tired body over to the surprisingly comfortable leather couch, I find myself content to just lie back and listen to Saint clean up in the kitchen. There's something so domestic about the way the dishwasher hums and the fridge gently opens and closes with each ingredient being put back in its rightful place.

Saint reemerges from the kitchen, drying his hands on a small dishtowel. "How are you feeling?"

"I'm all right." I release a slow exhale, and

Saint continues to appraise me, almost like he's inspecting me to be sure I'm telling him the truth.

"I've never really, uh, been around someone who's pregnant before. Are there, like rules, or . . ."

I grin, despite myself. "There are *some* rules. I'm not supposed to eat sushi or deli meats. I can't take certain medications. And there's some activities to avoid, like the obvious ones—bungee jumping, or even taking up a new vigorous workout routine."

"Darn, I'll have to cancel that skydiving excursion I was planning to take you on." He treats me to a wolfish grin.

I chuckle, appreciating yet again his easy sense of humor. "Trust me, you've done more than enough. I fact, I think I overdid it today," I say with a sigh. "My feet are pretty swollen."

"That sounds like fun," Saint says, somehow managing to sound both sarcastic and compassionate at the same time.

"Yeah, well, comes with the territory of being a mom-to-be. Here, let me make room for you," I mumble, trying to swing my feet off the couch, but Saint beats me to it, lifting them gently and placing them on his lap as he sits down.

I hold my breath. I don't care if he is a new friend—if I'm about to get a free foot massage from a handsome guy, I'm not about to say no.

"May I?" Saint asks, thumbs at the ready and poised against the soles of my feet.

I giggle a little and nod, words escaping me.

Wow, this guy is unreal. I'm half expecting to wake up from this wild dream—you know, the one where a magical stranger fulfills all my needs? But he digs his thumbs into my sore feet, and I don't wake up. Instead, I shudder in pleasure, stifling the moan that's begging to climb out of my throat.

This is intimate. Maybe too intimate. But I don't want it to stop.

"You have any siblings?" I ask, my mind blank.

What is this, speed dating?

"Only child," he says. "People tell me I give off only-child energy."

"Not at all." Genuinely surprised, I smile at him. "I would have guessed you were an older sibling with all of these caretaker instincts."

Saint laughs, and I notice—not for the first time—how broad his shoulders are. How deep his dimples are in his cheeks, and how defined his jawline is. I can't help but watch those muscular arms move, tapering down into thick, masculine hands. It's hard to ignore how devastatingly handsome my new friend is. And sweet, and attentive—

Okay, seriously . . . stop, Kinley. He's not interested in a chick who's seven months pregnant, and you're certainly not in the market for a new man.

"You have any siblings?" he asks, interrupting my inappropriate thoughts.

"One older brother. He actually lives—"

Saint hits a particularly ticklish spot, and I gasp.

"Sorry." He chuckles. "You good?"

The smirk on his lips sends a shiver of pleasure up my legs and into my core, coiling between my hips.

Okay, I'm turned on, I'll admit it, but there's no way in hell I'd let him know that. This man has been nothing but good to me, and I'm not about to make it weird by coming on to him. I'm pregnant, for Pete's sake. It's probably just hormones. And I certainly wouldn't want to risk the only friendship I've made here in Boston by being completely inappropriate with him.

"I'm good. Thank you." As I gently pull my feet back, I immediately miss the feel of his warm, strong hands soothing me. "I should probably go back to my place and unwind for the night. This was honestly such a nice day. Thank you."

"I had a good time too."

Why does this feel like the kind of conversation you have after a really great first date?

Almost as if he can read my mind, Saint asks, "Can I give you my number?"

"Um. Sure."

"Just in case you need anything before we hit up the farmers' market."

"Right. Just in case." I can't help the grin on my face.

I'm so out of practice that I don't even know if the man is flirting with me or just being considerate to a new neighbor. It's probably the latter. I could imagine Saint doing the same thing if an eighty-year old woman had moved in down the hall, carrying her groceries and boxes of books.

We exchange phone numbers quietly, and I try to ignore how my body is humming with excitement. I manage to convince him to let me walk back to my condo by myself, which is silly since I'm only down the hall.

"I'll see you later," I say. "Thanks again for today."

Saint leans against the door frame, his long and lean body on full display. It takes everything in me not to check him out.

"Thanks for dinner. Good night, Kinley."

"Good night."

Back at my place, my phone buzzes, and I half expect to see Saint's name. But the caller ID informs me it's someone else. *Mom*.

Oh boy. Here we go.

"Hey, Mom, what's up?"

"Hello, Kinley. I texted you earlier today and didn't hear back from you. It's like you want me to be worried sick."

"I'm sorry. I was out with a friend running errands."

"A friend? I didn't know you had friends in Boston."

"Well, he's kind of my first friend here, a neighbor from down the hall. Really sweet guy. He's kind of helped me out with Walker gone on his trip."

Mom huffs. "I still can't believe your brother left you like that. So irresponsible."

I roll my eyes.

My mom is impossible to please. Once you think you've achieved her expectations for you, she moves the goalpost. It doesn't help now that I'm pregnant with no partner in the picture. Which, in her words, is something I should be very embarrassed about.

"Walker worked really hard all year. He deserves a break. And like I said, the guy down the hall—"

"Guy down the hall?" Her tone is incredulous.

I feel suddenly defensive of Saint. "Yeah. He's really been helpful."

"You're not thinking of starting a relationship with this 'guy down the hall,' are you? Kinley, you just met the man. I swear, every time I think you've learned from your mistakes, you go and make things difficult for yourself all over again."

I clench my teeth tightly before forcing a smile. "Mom, it's fine. I'm not trying to get into another relationship right now."

My mother is quiet on the other end of the line for a moment. "That's good. I'm just worried about you, you know? With the baby coming . . . I just don't want to see you get hurt again. What kind of man would want you right now, anyway?"

Her words hit me like a slap to the face. "Wow, Mom. That's a really thoughtful thing to say to your single daughter."

"You know I didn't mean it like *that*, Kinley." She sighs, sounding so inconvenienced by my hurt feelings.

Mom is right, though. The last thing I need is some rebound fling. Although if you were going to have a rebound the strapping, sexy Saint would be the perfect man for the job. God, could you imagine?

"How's the baby?" Mom asks.

Changing the topic, I see. This woman is impossible.

Trying to calm myself, I take a deep breath. "Everything's good. I have an appointment with my new doctor this week."

"Well, let me know what your doctor says, all right? And please respond to my texts. I don't want to spend the whole day imagining what awful things could have happened to you. My single pregnant daughter alone in a big city."

"I'll call you as soon as I'm done," I tell her.

"All right. I love you, Kinley. Talk soon."

"'Bye, Mom."

My anxious pacing has led me to my bedroom, where I toss my phone on my bed. I flop down next to it, wiping angry tears from my eyes.

Gotta hand it to my mom for always knowing how to make a girl feel like crap on a cracker. She isn't wrong, though. I need to keep my priorities straight right now, and focus on settling into a new city and getting ready to become a parent for the very first time.

The little guy gives me a soft kick, and I place my hand over the spot, feeling him move inside me. The only man I have time for is this kung-fu master.

My phone buzzes. When I pick it up to see a text from Saint, my heart involuntarily squeezes.

You make it home okay?

I almost laugh. Of course I made it home okay. It was, what, a dozen steps?

But after talking to my mom, I'm sure I've read this situation all wrong. Saint is probably just taking pity on his poor, pregnant neighbor and generally being a good person. It was stupid of me to fantasize otherwise. He's gorgeous and definitely not interested in me like that. I'm lucky to have anyone around to support me right now. One small blessing, I guess.

I type out a response, my thumb hovering over the **SEND** icon while I read it over and over again.

> Made it down the hall in one piece miraculously. Thanks for caring. :-)

I huff out a sigh, deleting the text and opting for a simple thumbs-up emoji, then send it before I can obsess any more. Now isn't the time to flirt over text. I'm not some horny teenager anymore, crafting the perfect text to the boy I like.

It's time to act like an adult.

5

SAINT

Saturday, the farmers' market is brimming with people—young couples crowding around the booths and stands, little kids running wild around their parents' legs, dogs panting in the sun.

I'm not gonna lie, this is the kind of scene I feel like a total outcast in. Don't get me wrong, I love a day spent outside, and I'm not one to shy away from a crowd. But as soon as there are children underfoot, I feel like I've stumbled into Oz, and I'm one wrong step away from tripping over a munchkin. Maybe it's that I'm too big, or because I never know what to say to little people, but I'm outside my comfort zone for sure.

Kinley, on the other hand, is totally in her element. In a sporty outfit with a tote bag slung over her shoulder, she looks like just about any other young mom out here. Well, that's not entirely true. We've established that Kinley isn't just any mom; she's a *hot* mom.

With a pink halter top that accentuates her cleavage and a pair of maternity yoga pants stretched high over her round belly, Kinley is like a modern-day fertility goddess. Not to mention her long dark ponytail poking out of the back of her baseball cap.

God, I love a woman with a ponytail. Perfect for grabbing onto when—

A little girl with curly blond hair runs in front of us, halting my filthy thoughts as I almost trip over her.

"Munchkins," I mutter under my breath.

Kinley turns to me with an amused smile. "Watch out there, BFG. Tiny humans are afoot."

Chuckling, I shake my head at her. Different franchise, but *damn*, does this woman get my sense of humor. I shoot her a lopsided grin, but she's busy watching the little girl climb into her dad's arms with a fond smile.

My chest tightens with anxiety as I eye the guy who's signed his freedom away to a tiny snot-faced warden. I guess he looks pretty happy about it, though, doesn't he?

It still hasn't hit me that Kinley is going to have one of those soon. We haven't talked much about how she's feeling about all that, and I'm certainly no poet when it comes to sharing thoughts and feelings, so I haven't brought it up.

I lead us toward a colorful stand offering just about every shade of the rainbow in organic produce. Kinley does that cute little squirm she does when she's excited as she looks over the options. Standing behind her with one hand gripping the metal piping of the awning, I'm able to keep other shoppers from crowding her space. I'm also blocking the sun that's creeping under the tent so she doesn't overheat. It's nice to use my bulk for something other than hockey for once.

Perplexed, I watch as she inspects the dragon fruit with an appraising look. I wouldn't have the foggiest idea about what to do with a dragon fruit.

"Those plums look delicious," I murmur into her ear, not realizing how close my lips are to her skin until I feel my own breath bounce off her cheek.

She looks up at me with wide eyes, realizing how close we're standing, and points to a particularly shiny plum among the duller ones.

"That one?" I ask, plucking it from the selection when she nods.

I hold it out to her, but when she reaches for it, I whip my hand back with a smirk and take a big juicy bite. Kinley's eyes go wide as she glances at the vendor, who's busy with another customer. She shakes her head at me like a true mom, but there's a youthful giddiness in her smile.

I hold the plum back out to her, offering her the unbitten side. But instead of taking it, Kinley wraps her hand around my wrist, her fingers locked against my pulse. Then she leans forward and presses her pink lips to the dark fruit, penetrating the skin with her teeth and sucking the juices into her mouth.

All the while, our eyes are locked in an unspoken game of *who will break eye contact first.*

I sure as hell won't. Even though I know for a fact my pulse jumped from zero to arrhythmia, and she most definitely can feel my blood banging away beneath the skin of my wrist, I don't care. I love a challenge, especially when my contender is as sexy as Kinley.

All too soon, she pulls back with a devilish giggle and slowly chews the fruit. And just when I think I'm about to cream my pants, her tongue darts out from between her glossy lips to catch a droplet of sticky nectar from her chin.

Fucking hell. That was hotter than any blow job I've ever gotten.

"You're right. That's delicious," Kinley says with a satisfied hum before she turns away from me, swaying her hips as she walks down the grassy aisle to peruse the other stands.

I know I'm standing dumbstruck with a half-eaten plum steadily dripping down my arm, but I can't seem to make my feet budge. Pretty sure the moment I do, my growing hard-on is gonna make it really difficult to walk.

Kinley turns around, a smirk on those sexy lips. "You coming?"

Goddamn. This woman knows exactly what she's doing.

I slide a couple of dollars onto the stand and follow her lead. I can't wait to see what she'll do with a cucumber.

• • •

It's been a minute since I've seen the guys, so when Alex texts the group chat asking if anyone is up for a few rounds at the golf simulator downtown, I'm the first to respond.

Once I've dropped Kinley off at home and helped her unload our market haul, I check my phone for the address. When my gaze lands on a text in the group chat, my jaw tightens at the name. It's Reeves, saying he'll be there. I guess my number one fan is back from the Gulf of Mexico.

Well, I've been nothing but a Precious Moments angel since our fun little chat about my behavior. He won't have any reason to give me shit tonight. At least, he'd better not.

After I pay for parking, I find the place nestled between a restaurant and a sports equipment store. My clubs clink together in the bag slung over my shoulder as I descend the steps into the underground space. Alex and Tate wave to me from a collection of sofas in front of a giant screen that features a virtual course.

"Hey, man, glad you could come," Alex says, clapping me on the back twice.

Tate lifts a bottle of beer in greeting. "We just ordered a few buckets—you want a drink?"

I contemplate the offer, but knowing that Reeves could show at any second, I decide not to press my luck. "Nah, I'm good. What round are you on?"

One by one, the guys arrive with their clubs, and soon we're a party of five sprawled across three couches. I forgot how loud we can be when we're all together. Some might say we're a chatty bunch, shooting the shit like we do. Even Reeves is laughing, which is a bit out of character for him.

Speaking of which, Reeves has a tan. Good for him. I wonder if all that time in the sun thawed the frigid tundra of his soul. I notice him clock me over Lucien's shoulder as they swap vacation stories, and his smile settles into a frown.

Figures.

"Hey, man, how's it going?" I ask as he approaches me, his arms crossed over his chest.

"I'm good. The Gulf was awesome. I tried kiteboarding for the first time," he says, pausing before asking, "What have you been up to?"

There it is. The question on everyone's lips. *What havoc has Saint wreaked lately?*

"Oh, you know. Just keeping it simple."

"Good." The way he says it is almost like a threat.

The hairs on the back of my neck start to bristle

as I feel conflict brewing. "What, you don't believe me?"

A muscle jumps in his jaw. "I haven't seen anything in the tabloids since I got back, and neither has Coach. So either you're doing what you were told, or you're keeping it all under the table. Time will tell, I guess."

Doing what you were told. Like I'm some child who needs to be disciplined. This fucker knows he's getting on my last nerve, and yet he still keeps pushing my buttons.

"Yeah, all my debauchery is real hush-hush now," I say, waggling my eyebrows and placing one finger perpendicular to my lips. "Don't tell Dad, okay?"

Reeves sighs deeply, as if I'm the cause of all of his problems. "You know that if I learn anything, *anything* at all, I have to tell Coach. And if I tell Coach, then—"

"I'm suspended, yeah. I heard you loud and clear the first time," I grumble, shaking my head. I sound like a damn teen arguing with my parent about getting grounded.

Fuck this.

I break eye contact, instead choosing to stare

at one of the beer buckets. Since I got suspended, I haven't had a sip of alcohol, for no reason other than I haven't had a taste for it. One beer sounds real nice right now, though. Honestly, a whole bucket and a bender sounds great.

Reeves sighs again, understanding that the conversation is over. He moves to the farthest couch to talk to Lucien again.

Thank fuck. If I never have to have that conversation ever again, it will still be too soon.

"You're up." Alex nods to the screen before noticing my dark expression. "Whoa, you good?"

"I'm great," I say, masking my frustration with an easy smile. It's what I do best. Bury that shit deep and plaster a smile on my face.

I launch off the couch and grab my driver, taking a deep breath as I line up my shot. "Fore," I bellow, whacking the ball into the virtual green and delivering an Oscar-worthy performance of cheerfulness at the same time.

Alex claps me on the back while Tate says, "Nice shot, dude."

Lucien steps up behind me with a sly smile. "I'm coming for you, Saint."

I grin back. Isn't everyone these days?

. . .

The night dies down, and I somehow make it back to my condo without going off on a bender.

As I unlock the front door, my phone buzzes in my pocket. Anticipating a check-in text from Alex, I reluctantly pull it out and read it in the dark of my living room.

I'm still dreaming about that plum. Will you take me back next week?

Kinley. An irrepressible smile spreads across my face, more genuine than all the other smiles I put on tonight. I text back with fast, certain fingers.

I'll take you every week if you want me to.

Without skipping a beat, she texts back—nothing but a red kiss emoji.

My chest swells, the weight of the night's events evaporating into nothing. Just like that, my night has turned a complete one-eighty. And two texts from Kinley was all it took.

I'll be damned.

6

SAINT

Over the past couple of weeks, eating dinner with Kinley has become a regular event. There's usually some sort of reason behind each occasion. For starters, dinner is easier to make for two people, rather than paring ingredients down to a single serving. Once, I suggested we share a pizza so I didn't eat the whole thing by myself.

But behind each very practical purpose of spending time together, there's an unspoken understanding. We just like each other's company. She's definitely a cool girl, and I've enjoyed getting to know her.

Tonight, though, Kinley insisted on cooking for us, this time on the basis of needing to cook some shrimp that's been sitting untouched in her fridge.

I don't need convincing, but her invitation is still one of the funniest texts I've ever gotten.

come over and let me feed you some crustaceans that are going to exact their revenge if I don't cook them soon.

I text her back with a shrimp emoji, a drooling face, and a little blond running guy. She knows exactly what I mean, responding with a clock as if to say, *hurry.*

Texting with emojis is probably juvenile, but with Kinley, it's like a game. Our minds are on the same wavelength more often than not, so we can communicate with a couple of symbols rather than typing out full messages. And even when I'm not sure what she's saying, decoding the message is half the fun.

It's not a date, but I still strip out of my smelly workout clothes, take a quick shower, and spritz a little cologne across my bare chest. I contemplate wearing a button-up and dress pants, but ultimately decide to wear a simple cotton T-shirt and dark-wash jeans. I'm not sure where things are going with Kinley, but for once, I'm trying to just go with the flow and not worry about it.

A short walk down the hall, and I'm knocking on her door. Inside, I hear her yell, "Come in," and so I step over the welcome mat and through the unlocked door. She's done a lot of organizing this past week and the place looks fantastic.

"Wow, it's looking great in here. You got the TV set up. I told you I'd help with that."

"It's not even that big," she calls from the kitchen.

I follow the smell of sauteed shrimp until I'm hovering over Kinley as she works at the stove.

Maybe I should have dressed up more. She's wearing a black cotton dress that hugs her hips and cuts off at her knees. Over the dress is a light gray T-shirt knotted just above her belly bump, supporting her round breasts. Her hair falls in lazy waves down her shoulders, brushing against her bare arms. On her feet are those plush slippers I bought her at the supermarket. It's a casual outfit, but the way she wears it makes her look like a damn celebrity.

When Kinley looks up at me with a soft smile, it takes everything in me not to plant a kiss on her inviting lips. This woman exudes wife energy, and the fact that the little guy growing in her belly technically belongs to another man doesn't even faze me.

Okay, record scratch.

What's happening to me? Acknowledging my attraction to a woman is one thing, but playing house in my head? Clearly, I'm losing it.

Maybe it's because I haven't had sex in so long, my pent-up sperm count is fucking with my brain. Is that even a thing? Probably not. But I have no other explanation for my growing fascination with this woman.

Kinley yelps when grease splatters from the pan and lands on her arm, snapping me out of my weird thoughts.

"You okay?" I ask, reaching for a towel and wetting it under a cold stream of water in the sink.

Even as she insists she's fine, I gently take her arm and place the wet towel over the spot. It's a reflex, like my body is moving to protect hers without a single thought crossing my mind. It would weird me out if it didn't feel so natural.

"Thank you," Kinley says with a grateful smile. "Food is just about ready. Why don't you pour yourself a glass of wine?"

That doesn't sound like a bad idea. Do I break my brief stint with sobriety tonight?

As I pause, thinking it over, Kinley notices. "Do you not drink? That's totally okay if—"

"I do, I do. I just haven't for a few weeks. More for work reasons than anything else. One too many drinks, and I struggle to be on my best behavior."

When I don't elaborate, Kinley doesn't push. She just quirks an eyebrow at me and offers a sultry smile.

"An angel like you? I can't even imagine."

I shrug innocently. "That's what I've been saying."

"Well, it's probably for the best that you don't drink," Kinley says. "I'd just get jealous and spend all night groaning about how much pregnancy sucks."

All night. Is that an invitation to stay past dinner? "More than you usually do?"

She bumps me with her hip—a challenge. "Shut up. I haven't even told you the worst of it."

"Yeah? I'm all ears."

She taps her chin, a gesture I've learned she does when she's pretending to think very hard. "We'll see if you can handle it."

A few minutes later, we're cozied up on the couch together, enjoying the shrimp primavera Kinley whipped up from scratch. It's light, not as hearty as the pasta dishes I'm used to when I'm trying to bulk up, but it's hitting the spot.

Kinley's excited about the new TV, so we put on an oldie but a goodie, *Ferris Bueller's Day Off*. While a young Matthew Broderick spouts off one of his monologues, I turn to Kinley with a question.

"Now, tell me. What's the worst part about being pregnant?"

She finishes off her last bite with a giggle and sets our plates aside.

"Um, well," she mumbles before pulling a blanket over her knees, her toes peeking out to brush against my leg. "It's embarrassing. I don't want to say it."

"Okay, fine. You don't have to say it. I'll just guess until I get it right. Is it . . . your feet hurting?"

I touch her toes, dragging my fingers up her foot to rest my hand on her ankle. Between giggles, Kinley pantomimes zipping her lips and throwing away the key.

"Come on. At least nod or shake your head."

She sighs, and a reluctant smile curls at the corners of her mouth. "Fine."

"So, feet?"

She shakes her head.

All right then. I think back on everything she's said over the past few weeks, from her aching back to her fatigue.

"Difficulty sleeping?"

She taps her finger against her chin again before nodding slowly. "Warmer."

"All right," I say, adjusting my hand on her ankle so that it sits higher on her calf, rubbing the muscle there.

She sighs, leaning into the touch. "Even warmer," she murmurs. Then her eyes go wide and a blush crawls over her cheekbones, almost like she didn't mean to say that out loud.

Interesting.

I trail my fingers up and down her leg, enjoying how silky smooth her skin feels against my fingertips. "Something to do with your legs?"

She shrugs.

"Your . . . skin?"

She shrugs again.

"You gotta help me out here."

"Fine." She sighs dramatically, adjusting her position so that she's sitting closer to me on the couch. "But you have to promise not to make fun of me. Because it's *bad*."

"I promise."

Kinley and I enjoy poking fun at each other, but I would never intentionally tease her about something she's sensitive about. Still, I doubt it's actually something *bad*. I'm convinced she's over-reacting.

She stares at me with skeptical eyes, offering her pinky. "Pinky swear."

Solemnly, I accept her pinky, locking our fingers together. Neither of us lets go. She bites her lip, her eyes hooded with whatever secret she's too embarrassed to share with me.

"I swear. Now tell me."

Kinley meets my eyes, and the stormy expression on her face sends a rolling wave of desire down my body, gathering in the stiffness beneath my jeans. My hand stills on her leg, my nerves building.

"I'm pregnant, but I'm still human, right? And all these hormones raging through me are impossible to ignore. So that means I have certain . . .

wants. Needs, even." The tip of her tongue darts out to wet her lower lip.

I don't need emojis to know exactly what she's talking about. This message couldn't be clearer.

Kinley has been horny.

Which is pretty much the least helpful information ever. Because it's not like I can help her out of this jam.

"What's so bad about that?" I stare at her lips, my imagination running at breakneck speed.

They must be so soft. I want to feel them against my lips. Hell, I want to feel them on my—

"Because it's pointless." She focuses on her lap, the sparkle dulling in her eyes.

"Why?"

Looking up, she levels me with a stare. "Because who would want me like this?"

The question stuns me. I blink a few times, waiting for the punch line. But for once, Kinley isn't kidding.

Oh my God, she's dead serious. She thinks she's unattractive like this. Unlovable. Is she insane? My dick is halfway to hard right now and she's doing nothing but frowning at me.

"Kinley." I reach out, my hand still pinky-laced with hers, to lift her chin. "You wanna know something?"

Our mouths are only a breath apart, tempting fate. She looks up at me through her eyelashes.

"Tell me," she says, repeating my words from just moments earlier.

"*I* want you like this."

The words come easily, like I've said them to her a thousand times before. But I haven't. This is new, exhilarating in just how *right* it feels.

"You're just saying that to be nice," she says softly.

I shake my head. "I'm not, actually. You're beautiful. Sexy."

"That's not . . ." Her eyes shine with emotion, and the blush on her cheeks grows rosier.

"You are," I murmur.

"Saint . . ."

I stop her by pressing my lips to hers, sealing our mouths together in a chaste kiss. Kinley whimpers against me, reaching a small hand around my neck to pull me closer. And when she opens her mouth to my curious tongue, I welcome the chase.

This has been a long time coming, and as much as I want to take it slow, to learn what makes her shiver, we're both hungry.

I moan when she drags her fingernails against my scalp, reveling in the pleasure of it. When my hand ventures up her leg, she pushes her hips into my touch, daring me to go further. I worry that I'm crowding her when I guide her back against the pillows, but Kinley clings to me, starving for the connection of our lips, our hips.

My erect cock strains against the zipper of my jeans, begging for attention. Kinley is just as desperate, shoving the blanket between us to the floor and wrapping her toned legs around my pelvis, drawing me into her.

My curious hands have pushed her dress up over her hips, my fingers hungry to explore all the silky smoothness her body has to offer me. When my fingers brush the underside of her breast, Kinley gasps.

I break our kiss. "Wait," I say, my voice coming out strained.

"Wait?"

I've never been the type of guy to stop a good time, so my words surprise even me. But the need to check in with her wins out.

"This is . . . are you sure about this?"

She answers me with a kiss. A kiss so hot that I groan at the sensual strokes of her tongue touching mine.

When I caress her breasts over her shirt, she shifts.

"You can take it off," she says, and my dick twitches possessively in my jeans.

With a nod, I help her lift both the shirt and the dress underneath up and over her shoulders, until she's curled beneath me with nothing on but a pair of lacy underwear and a matching bra.

"Take yours off too," she murmurs, her voice breathy as her fingers skirt along the waistband of my jeans, flirting with the grooves in my ab muscles.

When I pull my T-shirt over my head in one swift movement, her eyes widen, drinking me in.

"Wow. Your body is insane."

As much as I enjoy her attention, I'm suddenly very preoccupied, lowering over her to press my lips against her neck—new territory to explore. Kinley bucks with pleasure, tightening her legs around my hips until the bulge in my pants is flush with her heat. I can feel her burning through my jeans.

Oh hell.

I trail kisses down her breasts, pulling the fabric away greedily to see her rosy nipples, peaked with excitement and ready for my eager mouth. When my lips brush against the sensitive skin there, Kinley shudders and grips my shoulders tightly.

Note to self: Kinley's breasts are very, *very* sensitive.

I tease her nipple with my tongue, drawing lazy circles until her moans crescendo into gasping cries. Sucking her breast into my mouth, I grind my hips between her legs, feeling her writhe beneath me.

"Please, Saint, I—" Her voice is shaky as she pushes helplessly at the hem of her panties.

Yes, ma'am.

It's easy for me to pull the thin lace down her legs. It's easy for me to part her legs and gaze at the sweet, glistening nirvana waiting for me there. It's easy for me to unbutton my jeans, reach inside, and pull out my aching member and rub it once, twice . . .

What's not so easy is the nagging notion that Kinley is pregnant.

I've never had sex with a pregnant woman. Are there dos and don'ts I'm not familiar with? Is the baby going to be okay if we go and move around the furniture in there?

Fuck, I didn't even bring a condom. Amateur.

Kinley looks at me with big, worried eyes. "Is something wrong?"

"Nothing."

I lean down and kiss her lightly on the lips, soothing her. No point in dwelling on my lack of planning now. One thing I do know is that a little cunnilingus never killed anyone. I coax her mouth open with my tongue, kissing her deeply before I trail my lips down her cleavage and over her belly.

Soon, my kisses move between her legs until my tongue is poised at her clit. She tilts her hips, and I lick and suck firmly against her. She tastes like heaven. Kinley is groaning now, *loudly*, rocking her hips against my needy mouth as I taste her.

"Don't stop, don't stop, yes, yes, yes—"

I suck her tight little bud into my mouth, flicking my tongue against it until I feel Kinley's legs tense around my head, her pelvis shaking erratically with the force of her orgasm.

"Saint, oh my God." She gasps, her voice

catching as she laughs breathlessly. "Best neighbor ever."

We both laugh at that, and I crawl up her body to press a kiss against her damp forehead. "Happy to be of service."

"Help me up," Kinley says, and so I offer her both my hands and pull her upright. She gives me a deliriously happy grin and smacks a big, fat kiss to my lips. "Thank you."

"You're very welcome."

"Now it's your turn."

"No, you don't—"

"Are you really about to say no to this?"

She gives me an unimpressed look, and I relent with a sheepish smile. I lean back, raising my hands in defeat. But if this is defeat, I'm happy to be a loser any day of the week. Because the idea of Kinley's sweet mouth on my cock? Well, that's just the best thought ever.

"Have at it."

And she does. Holy fucking hell, she does.

With some cushions under her knees, Kinley climbs off the couch and nestles between my legs. There's no nervous fumbling, no tentative strokes.

Instead, she immediately puts me in her mouth, and I let out a loud groan.

Her mouth is hot and wet, and wow, how did she learn that trick with her tongue?

She engulfs most of my shaft in her mouth, the rest in her spit-slick hand. When she pulls back, she drags her tongue across the head, teasing it with her lips.

"Fucking hell, Kinley." I stare down at her in wonder.

This girl. With my manhood utterly at her whim, Kinley is giving it her absolute all.

It's been a while since a woman looked at me the way she's looking at me right now. I shudder when she takes me in deep again, feeling my own orgasm creeping up on me. She's confident and determined and, wow, I'm way too close.

"Kin, I'm gonna come if you want to—"

But she doubles down, locking her lips against me and sucking, using her hand to jerk me off the rest of the way. I touch her hair, then lean my head back, and the sound I make is damn near animalistic. I may as well be one with the way she's milking me and swallowing it all down with a satisfied hum. I come so hard, I think I see spots.

"Goddamn." I reach for Kinley, my eyes closed with exhaustion. Once I catch her hands, I pull her back onto the couch, where she sprawls over me, resting her head on my shoulder.

She giggles lightly, pressing a kiss to my knuckles. "This would be a lot more comfortable for me if we moved to the bed. You can stay the night if you want."

A bolt of surprise flashes through me. I love how easygoing she is. There are no games, no guesswork, no awkward *what do we do now* moments.

"Uh, yeah. Sure."

Kinley pats me on the cheek before she gets up, turning off the forgotten movie and gathering her discarded clothes. I watch her butt wiggle as she walks away, and damn, is it cute.

I tug my jeans into place since I'm still sitting here with my dick out. Not my finest moment, but shit, I think she almost sucked the life out of me.

"I'm going to take a shower. Come and join me once you've reentered the land of the living." She presses her lips to mine in a quick peck before her footsteps fade down the hallway to the bathroom.

When the pipes creak and the shower starts, I

open my eyes. A goofy, satisfied smile stretches across my lips.

I've never stayed the night with a woman, on principle. I usually don't want to give anyone false hope.

But with Kinley . . . I know it's not like that. And I have no intention of making the trek back to my place, even if it's just a few short strides down the hall. Things are different with her.

For the first time in a while, I'm just going to do what feels right.

• • •

"Good morning," I whisper against Kinley's hairline, enjoying the way she grumbles in response.

"What time is it?" she asks, her eyes bleary. She looks absolutely heavenly, all sleep-rumpled and drowsy. Seeing the cup of hot tea in my hand, she smiles. "Mmm. Can I have some of that?"

"You can have it all. I have my own," I say.

As I help her sit up, she blinks over at the morning light peeking through the drawn curtains and squints against the sun.

"Oh God, you're a crazy early bird, aren't you?" She gives me a look of disgust over the edge of the teacup, like she's willing to end this summer fling on the basis of my sleeping habits.

"Easy." I chuckle, shooting her a sly wink. "Wait until you hear about breakfast."

"What about breakfast?" At first she's skeptical, but then she sniffs the air and gasps. "Is that bacon?"

When I nod, Kinley sighs happily. I chuckle at her adorable enthusiasm.

I'm an early riser because of the years I've spent going to early morning practices. Meanwhile, Kinley sleeps like a rock. Once we snuggled into bed together last night after another make-out sesh in the shower, she knocked out.

Spooning her with my hand splayed across her belly, I was content to listen to her soft breathing until I fell asleep. I'm aware how weird that sounds, but it was more calming than any melatonin supplement I've ever tried.

At one point, I woke up, feeling the little guy kick against my hand. It was a strange reminder that it's not just Kinley and me in this bed. She has a baby on the way. Even though I'm sure he'll be a great kid, I have zero idea how I'll fit into Kinley's life once he's here.

A sinking feeling settles inside me. I guess it's a knot I'll have to unravel later.

Now, at the table, her pregnant belly is on full display under her tiny pajama top. She runs her hand absentmindedly over the taut skin as she fills her plate with bacon, scrambled eggs, and sliced strawberries.

"You're unreal, you know that?" Kinley looks at me from across the table with a radiant smile, her fresh face beautiful, even without makeup.

"Right back atcha, gorgeous."

As we smile at each other like a couple of idiots, the moment is rudely interrupted by a rapid knocking at the door. Kinley glances at the clock and curses under her breath before looking at me apologetically.

"I forgot I was supposed to do breakfast with my brother."

"Is that him?"

My pulse spikes a bit. I didn't realize this would become a *meet the family* kind of situation so quickly. And by the way Kinley is staring blankly at the door, I don't think either of us really knows what to do in this moment.

"Yeah. If you don't want to meet him yet—"

"No, no, it's fine. Lemme go put a shirt on."

I lean over and press a kiss to the top of her head before retreating to the bedroom. I grab my T-shirt from the chair in the corner of her room. Once I'm dressed, I smooth my hair in the mirror, listening as Kinley opens the door and another man's voice echoes through the condo.

A familiar voice.

Dread creeps down my spine as I struggle to place it. Curious, I step out of the room and down the hall, until I'm standing face-to-face with none other than the Boston Titans' team captain, Walker Reeves.

Shit.

"Saint?" His eyes nearly pop out of his skull at the sight of me. "What are you . . ."

I look at Kinley a little helplessly, who is staring at us both with the sudden realization that her big brother and her new fuck buddy already know each other.

Good times.

"What's up, Reeves?" I say weakly.

Why is it that my life never ceases to be a goddamn circus? Why did I never give any thought to the fact that Kinley's last name is Reeves? What is it about me that attracts unbridled disaster?

His expression darkens as the gears in his head start to click, sparking a flurry of emotions behind his eyes. "Saint . . . what the *fuck* are you doing here?"

My clothes are rumpled, and I'm sure my hair is sticking up in like six different directions. There's no denying that I slept here, that Kinley and I just woke up.

"Walker . . ."

Kinley holds up a hand to stop her brother, stepping between us as he advances on me. He's looking at me like he'd love to beat the ever-loving shit out of me if I don't make a quick exit.

"I'll get out of here. Enjoy your breakfast." My words come out stiff and robotic as I grab my shoes and beeline for the door.

Who knows if I'll ever see Kinley again after this shitstorm, besides in awkward hallway run-ins. To spare my heart the hurt, I don't even give her a final glance.

"Saint, wait," she calls out.

The door clicks behind me before I can make

the decision to turn back and clear things up.

There goes the one good thing I had going for me. And probably my career too.

Well, fuck.

7

KINLEY

Walker swipes his credit card aggressively in the reader and pays for our drinks—a cold brew for him and an iced herbal tea for me.

The poor barista scurries away, probably terrified of the big burly man with the bad attitude. He shoves the card back in his wallet, grumbling about the price of cold brew these days. Ever since he walked in on Saint and me at the condo earlier . . . let's just say my brother hasn't been very *peppy* this morning.

"I could have paid for my own, you know," I mutter, poking him teasingly in his side.

"It's fine," he growls.

Sheesh. Hello, Mr. Grumpy Pants.

When Walker came back into my life and more or less saved my pregnant butt from financial ruin, I thought I was seeing a brand-new side of him. A kinder, gentler, more generous side. It was like he'd become a new man in the years we'd spent apart. Someone who had really gotten his life together and genuinely wanted to do right by his kid sister.

Now, *this* crabby old man? *This* is the Walker I remember from my childhood. Bossy. Dramatic. Protective to a fault.

"Well, thank you for the tea."

"You're welcome."

It's awkwardly silent for a few minutes while we wait for our drinks. Walker lets out a heavy sigh. He's acting like such a child.

How do I convince him that I'm an adult who is capable of making her own decisions? I've been on my own for so long, I haven't needed to prove my independence to anyone, except when Mom unexpectedly calls me and unloads all her pent-up judgment on my life. Then I feel like I have to defend all my life choices.

Gotta love family, right?

I tiptoe into this conversation like I'm dismantling a bomb. "So, do you want to talk about what your deal with Saint is, or—"

Walker turns to me, his eyes blazing. "Look, Kin, I don't know how many ways I can say it. Saint is a bad guy."

"I hear you, and I respect your position," I say, feeling like I'm talking to a disgruntled client. Or an angry toddler? I really hope toddlers aren't like this, since I'll be raising one pretty soon. "But that's just not been my experience with him."

"Right. Your *experience*. And I'm sure you've had a whole lot of that in the, what . . . three weeks you've lived here?" Walker shoots me a condescending look, and I glare at him in response.

No matter how utterly pissed off he is at me—at Saint, at this *whole* situation—I refuse to sink to his level and trade jabs with him.

"Can we please be adults here?"

"You're the one fucking my teammate behind my back like we're in high school again."

"High school? I *never* fucked—"

"Large iced hibiscus?" a small voice says from behind the counter. The barista holds out my pink-and-purple drink with a pinched look of well-placed worry.

If I didn't know Walker, I'd be worried about his behavior too. I look around to find the other customers side-eyeing us from the small tables and booths.

Okay, we're definitely making a scene. *Awesome*.

I smile politely and thank the barista before heading to the farthest corner of the coffee shop to wait for Walker to join me. Maybe he'll chill out once he's had a little caffeine. I'm wiping the condensation off the sides of my icy drink when he slumps into the seat across from me.

Sure enough, after a few sips, he starts to mellow.

"I just don't understand how this could have happened." Walker sighs, abandoning his anger for something a little more exhausted.

I almost feel bad for him. He's clearly distraught over this entire thing.

"We live in the same building, Walker. He found me trying to carry a heavy package and offered—"

"A package? I could have brought that up for you."

"Oh, and then you were gonna fly back to the

Gulf when you were done? Be realistic. I needed help in that moment, and Saint was there. There was nothing to it."

"Nothing?" Walker narrows his eyes. "What I witnessed this morning didn't look like *nothing*. It looked like a whole lot of *something*."

"You mean a fun night between two consenting adults? Then yeah, that was something."

A very nice something, but I can't let myself sink into the warm memories of Saint's hands—or mouth—right now.

My brother visibly shudders. "Come on, Kinley. I don't wanna hear about that."

Looks like I have to change my approach here. The only way I'm going to get through to him is by trying to relate to his situation.

How would I feel if Walker hooked up with one of my coworkers? One of my enemies? Not that I have any coworkers or enemies . . . but still, I don't blame him for feeling weird about it.

I take a deep breath and then another sip of tea. "Okay, I'll admit it. Things happening between me and Saint weren't planned. It all just sort of evolved."

Evolved. That's good, I decide. A very non-sexy

word for what took place in my condo last night.

"But I didn't know that he was on your team. He never mentioned hockey once." Come to think of it . . . is that weird?

Walker scoffs. "You expect me to believe that? That's usually his opening line, and girls all but fall into his bed."

I lick my lips and continue. "Look I get that you don't exactly think highly—"

"Kinley . . ." My brother's voice holds a warning.

"Drink some more of that." I tip my chin toward the coffee clutched in his massive hand. "You're a cranky bastard when you haven't had your caffeine."

As my brother obeys, I let out a little sigh.

"When I met Saint, as far as I knew, he was just the nice guy down the hall who was willing to lend a helping hand. He's been nothing but kind to me. With my current situation, I'd be a fool to look a gift horse in the mouth and say, 'No thank you, I'm good.'"

Walker cocks his head, appraising me coolly. "And why do you think he didn't tell you that he's a hockey player? Why did he hide that?"

Frowning, I pause. "I mean . . . I never really asked. All I knew was that he had the summer off, so we've been hanging out pretty much every day for the last few weeks."

"Every day? Jesus, Kinley. I thought you were smarter than this."

I reach across the table and flick his nose *hard*, just like I used to when we were kids. Walker swats my hand away with a frown.

"I *am* smart," I say, scowling at him, "and I also pride myself on having a good asshole radar. Which, by the way, is going crazy right now." I point accusingly at him.

So much for toning down the sass. *Take it down a notch, Kinley.*

"I'm just trying to look out for you," Walker says with a surprising amount of earnestness. "I know Saint, and I know his lifestyle. He's not the kind of guy you need in your life right now. He's just playing games."

Whether they're true or not, my brother's words sting. I feel a lump rising in my throat. *Freaking pregnancy hormones.*

"Mom more or less said the same thing." But I'd told myself that Mom didn't know Saint—

Walker does. That's a little more worrying than I'm willing to let on.

Walker's expression softens even more. "I just don't want you to get hurt, Kin."

"I know." I reach across the table and squeeze his hand. "Can we talk about something other than my sex life now? This isn't the best topic of conversation for siblings."

"Will you stop seeing Saint?"

"I—I don't know," I say, compelled for some reason to answer truthfully, and Walker's eyes harden again.

I don't want my relationship with my brother to be compromised by a silly hookup. And besides, I need to focus on the baby right now. I can't be inviting strange men into my bed every night.

Not that Saint is a stranger. Not anymore.

Ugh. This is gonna suck.

"I'll think about it, okay?"

Walker just nods, but I can tell there's a storm brewing behind his eyes. It's true that he knows Saint better than I do, or at least he's known him longer. I have to believe my brother when he says he just wants the best for me.

If only I knew what "the best for me" even looks like.

"Can we talk about literally anything else right now?" I beg. "Tell me about kiteboarding."

Walker's mouth lifts into an uneasy smile. "Sure."

• • •

"The baby is healthy as can be," Dr. Harding says with a cheerful grin, setting her clipboard on the laminate countertop. "Everything is looking perfect. How are you feeling?"

Exhausted. Instead of being truthful, I offer her a weak smile. "Oh, I'm okay."

The doctor tilts her head, her brow furrowed. "Are you feeling any stress?"

Stress? That's an understatement. With the baby on the way and everything going on with Walker and Saint, there's a circus of thoughts banging around in my head.

"No more than usual."

"The best thing you can do for yourself and the baby is to find a way to stay relaxed. Can I give you some personal advice?"

"Sure."

"If something is stressing you out during your pregnancy, it's best to distance it from your life as much as you can. For some women, that means taking time off from work. For others, it means rethinking some relationships. I, for one, had to set boundaries with my mother-in-law while I was pregnant. She was hovering more than a satellite."

I nod, soaking in her wisdom. Dr. Harding looks about two decades older than I am, with a few soft wrinkles around her eyes and gray strands in her dark hair. We've only seen each other a couple of times, but I already trust her implicitly.

"Was it hard to set those boundaries?" I ask, not sure who I'm thinking about setting them with. Walker? Saint? All of the above?

"Of course. But it gets easier. This is your first pregnancy, so give yourself some grace. What matters right now is you and your child. Everyone else and their opinions should come second."

As we share a warm smile, I blink away a prickling sensation behind my eyes. "Thank you, Dr. Harding. That's really helpful."

She squeezes my shoulder gently. "I'm glad.

Do you have a ride home?"

"Yeah, my brother's waiting outside."

She nods, but the solemn look in her eye makes me think she's catching on to the fact that my family life may be what's stressing me out so much. "That's good. I guess I'll see you in a couple of weeks. Take care, Kinley."

While I'm settling the bill with the front desk, my thoughts drift back to Saint. I want nothing more than to text him right now and give him an update on my day. I know he'll probably have some funny quip to make me laugh. But with all the drama that went down this morning, a casual text seems insensitive.

Dr. Harding said I should distance myself from the people who make my life hard, but Saint has made my life nothing but easier. More than being kind and lending a helping hand, Saint makes me laugh. Being with him makes me forget my discomfort. I don't even care about the little inconveniences of life when he's around. I know in my gut that he's a good man. Walker's judgment is just clouded by their dumb rivalry.

If I want Saint around, does that mean I have to distance myself from my brother?

"Everyone else and their opinions should come

second."

Walking out of the building and into the sun, I catch Walker's eye from where he's sitting in his car.

As he gives me a smile and waves out the window, I'm suddenly thrown back to a time long, long ago, when Walker taught me how to drive in our dad's old station wagon. I was a mess behind the wheel, slamming on the brakes every few seconds and constantly forgetting my turn signals. He was a jerk about it sometimes, sure, but he stuck through it for me because that's who Walker is—bossy, dramatic, and protective to a fault. Generosity isn't a new character trait of his. It's always been there, beneath the rough exterior.

"How'd it go?" he asks while I draw the seat belt over my belly.

Gosh, I'm getting big. "Everything's golden."

Walker reaches over and takes my hand, giving it a light squeeze, and my heart just about caves in with guilt.

I can't believe I was toying with the idea of choosing a silly summer fling over my new and improved relationship with my big brother. Yes, Saint is a great guy, and yes, the orgasms were outstanding, but I can't continue to be selfish. Not when family is on the line. Not with the little guy on the way.

No more playing around. It's time to focus on becoming the best mother I can be.

8

SAINT

This is probably the dumbest move I've ever made. After my life did what it always does—knock me on my ass with a heavy dose of irony—I retreated back to my place like a wounded puppy.

Learning that the woman I've been messing around with is my team captain's little sister should have been enough to shock some sense into me. Apparently, there's no sense in my head to begin with, because here I am, standing at Kinley's door with a big bag of Thai food and a store-bought cake with **SORRY** written on top in cursive lettering in bright yellow frosting.

It takes me an embarrassingly long time to dredge up the courage to knock. I'm nervous to see Kinley, but at least I'm man enough to admit that.

I also wouldn't put it past Reeves to be waiting behind his own door, only feet away from Kinley's, with a kitchen knife and every intention of ending me.

Straightening my shoulders, I knock a little loudly because I've always been a ballsy motherfucker. If Reeves wants a fight, he'll get one. I'm not about to let go of my connection with Kinley so easily.

The door opens.

"Saint . . ." Kinley breathes out my name, one hand resting protectively over her belly. She always does that when she opens the front door, whether she's aware of it or not. Must be a mama bear thing. She's protective of her belly, of the baby inside. It's kind of endearing.

Today she's wearing a blue cotton dress with quilted pockets and her hair is braided to one side. Any words I prepared dissolve into a puddle like ice cream on a summer day. She's stunning. Her eyes are bright and inquisitive, and somewhere deep inside them, I can tell that she's happy to see me—if not a little confused.

"What are you doing here?" She must have the same anxious thought as me, because her gaze darts over to her brother's door.

I hold out the food as a peace offering. "We had dinner plans."

Kinley gives me an unimpressed look. "I don't remember making plans."

I feign confusion. "I distinctly remember you saying that I could eat you out any night of the week."

Kinley flushes a bright shade of pink, holding the door open wider. "Oh my God, Saint. Shut up and get in here before he hears something."

"Yes, ma'am."

Inside, we take a moment to just stare at each other. It's only been ten or eleven hours since I saw her this morning, but this moment feels like something bigger.

Should I say something?

Eventually, Kinley breaks eye contact to peer suspiciously at the brown paper bag and plastic container in my hands. "Thai food?"

"You bet."

"And is that a cake?"

"Specially made."

A rogue smile pulls at her mouth. "Are you trying to bribe me?"

"Less of a bribe. More of an apology." I tilt the container so she can read the sugary message written in loopy cursive.

"Sorry? For what?" She takes it from me with genuine confusion in her eyes.

"For not telling you what I do for a living."

Kinley sighs softly. I can tell she's not mad at me, and my relief at that is instantaneous. "I'm really the one who should apologize. Walker was totally out of line this morning, and—"

"I didn't know he was your brother, for the record. If I did, I would have stayed far, *far* away."

She smiles softly. "Well then, I'm glad you didn't know. For the record."

We grin at each other, having fallen naturally back into our familiar conversational rhythm. Wordlessly, she leads me to the table where we set out the food and settle in together to eat.

Kinley moans through a mouthful of noodles. "How did you know I was craving exactly this?"

I shrug. "Something you said to me the first time we met. Lucky guess."

"The luckiest." She giggles, reaching out to

wipe a bit of sauce from my lower lip.

It feels so natural being this close to her, almost as if the last time we sat here didn't end with her brother almost vaulting over the table to strangle me.

"So," she says, pausing to pull the noisy plastic cover off the cake, "why didn't you tell me you played hockey? If you'd said that earlier, we would have been able to put two and two together much earlier on."

"When I tell a woman that I play hockey for a living . . ." I pause when her eyebrows lift, then clear my throat to start again. "Usually, when people figure out who I am, they look me up and immediately know everything there is to know about me. It's crazy what you can find online. My stats for the seasons, which teams I've played for. Where I was born. My height, my weight, my salary. It's all people want to talk about. It's all they care about. I didn't want it to be like that with you. You're new to the city and you didn't know who I was. It was nice to have a fresh start with someone."

Nodding, she gives me a soft look. "But eventually you were going to have to tell me."

"Yeah, eventually. But I wanted to keep you away from the tabloids while I got my life in order."

"Do the tabloids not like you?"

A little reluctantly, I chuckle. "No, they actually love me. I do a lot of stupid shit, which makes the team look bad. The tabloids have people who follow me around the city to clubs and bars and whatnot. That's why I've been laying low for the past month or so. It's part of the reason why your brother hates me so much."

"What's the other part?"

I shrug. "I'm prettier than he is."

Kinley snorts out a giggle. "That you are."

Her gaze lingers on mine, and I try to ignore the way my jeans grow tighter. Now is really *not* the time for an inappropriate boner.

"So, am I forgiven?" I do my best to sound casual, but a hint of desperation bleeds through.

I don't know what I'd do if Kinley cut me out of her life for good. I haven't had a connection with someone like this before, and I'm not about to lose it over some dumb hockey squabble.

"Of course. Cake heals all wounds."

The tightness in my chest eases a little, and I give her a grateful grin. Sure enough, eating the bakery-bought cake is an experience that's damn near spiritual.

I make the mistake of smearing a dollop of icing on Kinley's nose, which very quickly escalates to nearly getting a face full of cake myself.

I catch her hand, now covered in buttercream frosting, and draw her fingers to my mouth one by one to lick them clean. Kinley's giggles stop as she becomes breathless, her pupils wide. With a sexy little smirk, she smears some icing on her lips, an invitation I'd be a damn fool to reject.

We're a little sticky from the sugar, but it doesn't matter. There's nothing sweeter than Kinley's warm mouth. My tongue caresses hers, eliciting a heady moan that sends a wave of excitement down the back of my neck. My dick presses hungrily against my zipper as my hand wanders up the length of her leg, squeezing her thigh and pulling her close to me.

"I missed you today." She sighs between languid kisses along my jaw, her hands wandering the expanse of my shoulders.

I want to tease her, remind her we weren't separated for more than half a day, but her tongue must be laced with some sort of truth serum because I whisper, "I missed you too."

With that, I'm tugging Kinley into my lap, pressing our bodies together in an electric embrace. She rocks her hips against me, grinding against my swollen shaft, which is still shoved unpleasantly against my zipper.

"Am I too heavy?" she asks a little nervously.

"You're perfect."

Pulling away the straps of her dress, I occupy myself with the taste of her collarbones, her breasts, her perky little nipples. Kinley knots her fingers in my hair, leaning back in her pleasure to give me full access to wherever my lips choose to venture next. My hands are the real explorers, though, sliding beneath the thin cotton of her panties to cup her ass and squeeze.

God, this woman has a good ass.

"Let's move somewhere more comfortable," I say softly.

Panting, she nods. "The bedroom."

With one hand under her ass and the other around her waist, I stand and carry her toward her room.

Kinley's mouth presses to the stubble on my throat. "I can walk, you know."

I grunt out a reply, but I don't release her.

The feel of her firm belly pressing into me should feel strange, foreign . . . but it doesn't. I like the feel of her in my arms, and I appreciate all the parts of her body and what it can do.

When we reach the bed, I place her in the center of the mattress, and Kinley tugs me down with her. I chuckle and lie down with her in the center of the bed. We turn to our sides, facing each other.

I take her mouth in another searing kiss. Part of me knows I should put an end to this, but the other part of me wouldn't stop what we're doing for all the money in the world.

Her knees part, and I bring my hand beneath her dress to caress her over her panties.

Kinley gasps, her eyes glassy with desire. "Do you . . . have a condom?"

"No." I sigh, dipping my head to nip at her neck. "I wasn't sure how tonight would go, so I didn't . . ." My words trail off into a strangled groan as Kinley dips her hand into the front of my pants and palms me firmly.

"That's all right," she murmurs. "There's plenty we can do without one."

Deftly, Kinley unzips me, and the first touch

of her fingers to my cock sends a jolt of pleasure down my spine.

Half the pleasure is the feel of her soft fingers moving around me, barely able to encompass the full thickness of it. The other half is the way she looks getting me off, her dress pulled down low to reveal her flushed, naked chest.

The feeling is overwhelming, beyond temptation, so I let my hands do exactly what they want, one coming up to massage her breast and pinch her nipple, and the other sneaking beneath her dress to the warmth between her legs. With a gasp, Kinley opens her legs wider, allowing two of my curious fingers to plunge deep inside her.

"Oh wow . . ." She groans, her free hand clawing at the back of my neck for purchase.

As pleasure overtakes her, her hand's pace on my cock falters, but I don't care. If she keeps making noises like that, I'm going to lose a handle on my careful control.

At Kinley's trembling request, I thrust my fingers deeper and faster, crooking them just so. She's so warm, and I can't help but imagine what it'll feel like once I'm actually inside her, buried deep.

We lock eyes, and as if we're both thinking the same thing, Kinley shudders in my arms, her orgasm hitting her hard and relentless. Just the sight is enough to take me over the edge, and soon I'm coming into her hand with a rush of pleasure that makes me dizzy.

She crumples against me, resting her head on my shoulder while she catches her breath. Instinctually, I pull her into me, locking my arms around her waist. For a long time, there's nothing but the sound of our breathing filling the silence.

But these feelings welling up inside me? They're louder than any concerns knocking around in my head. So what if her crazy brother beats me bloody when he finds out we're still seeing each other?

For this woman, it might just be worth it.

9

KINLEY

I wake up to the sound of my phone buzzing faintly under my pillow. Through groggy eyes, I see the caller ID reads WALKER. I cringe, debating whether to pick up. It's barely nine in the morning, the psycho.

The call goes to voice mail before I can decide to answer it, my screen lighting up with not one but *three* missed calls and about a dozen text messages to boot.

What the hell is going on?

Bewildered, I reach across the sheets for Saint but find the other side of my bed empty. Down the hall, the pipes creak and the shower turns on. He's still here, at least.

Reluctantly, I pull myself upright to absorb

Walker's messages before I accidentally drift off again. They start from last night, around the time when Saint brought me dinner. The voice mails make me nervous, so I scroll through the texts first.

Hey Kin, wondering if you have any dinner plans. I'm thinking about making lasagna. I'll have lots of leftovers.

And about an hour later—

You okay?

I guess you fell asleep early. Give me a call when you wake up.

And then this morning—

Hey Kin. I knocked on Saint's door last night to talk to him, man to man. He didn't answer.

I checked this morning too.

Is he with you?

Kin the guy is bad news. You don't know his history.

My stomach sinks as I continue to read.

I could tell you myself but if you've googled him even once you should have a pretty good idea what he's really like.

Saint is already close to being suspended. I'm obligated to keep an eye on him, but I don't want to have to tell Coach he's fooling around with my little sister.

I've worked with him for years. If he is ultimately suspended, he'll spiral and you will get caught up in his shitstorm.

It's not worth it.

Kin, call me.

That's the end of the texts, and despite waking up in a happy mood, I press a hand to my stomach, which is starting to churn. I put my phone face-down on my lap and take a few deep breaths.

I want to cry. Or throw my phone against the wall. This is too much. Against my better judgment, I listen to the voice mails too.

"Hey, Kinley, I know it's early but I need you to call me back."

"Kin, I'm really worried about you. I didn't hear back from you last night. I thought about busting down your door, but I obviously didn't want to do that because that's crazy, for one, and also because I want to give you space to make your own decisions and live your own life. I just . . . call me back, okay? I feel like I'm losing my mind."

"Okay, officially starting to feel like a lunatic. Saint isn't home, so I have to assume the two of you are together. You said yourself that you've been spending every waking moment with him. I didn't think it through when I moved you in this building. I should have known. I'm really worried he's doing this to get some sort of revenge on me . . . I've always given the guy a hard time, and I may have taken it too far lately with his suspension on the table. I just don't want you to be sucked in when he goes off the deep end. Just call me so we can talk it out."

I don't know how long I've been staring at the wall when Saint walks back into the bedroom. He's bare-chested with a white towel wrapped low around his hips. A thick trail of steam follows him from the hall, fogging up my mirror.

"Good morning, sunshine," he says before seeing my expression. "Hey . . . what's going on? Are you okay?"

I meet his wide-eyed expression with an empty sigh. "Not really."

He kneels in front of me, droplets still clinging to his wet hair. "What is it? The baby?"

"No," I choke out. "I just can't do this anymore."

"Do what, sweetheart?"

"This was the last time. I'm so sorry."

"The last—"

"We can't see each other anymore."

"Kinley, if this is about your brother, I can talk to him. I can—"

I lean in and press a chaste kiss to Saint's full lips, savoring the way he automatically kisses me back. It's all too sudden, too dramatic. But this is the way it has to be, right?

Boundaries and all that. Doctor's orders.

Without another word, I climb out of bed and beeline toward the bathroom, closing the door behind me.

First, I pee for like forty-three years because that's just my life now. Then I crank the shower knob, letting the hot water steam up the room to sauna-like levels. I take a long shower—the kind you spend contemplating your life choices and where they've led you up to this point.

When I'm finally done, Saint is gone.

• • •

"It's too expensive," I say, holding up the price tag so Walker can take a better look. "Honestly, this is highway robbery."

After I met him at the coffee shop, my brother kindly offered to take me to the local baby supply store to pick out a car seat. I initially objected, reminding him that I don't even own a car. But then he reminded me that *he* has a car, adding that he's also going to get me my own car for my birthday, which is . . . just too much.

But if I know anything about my brother, it's that resistance is futile. You can't argue with the man. Unless you have the energy of a thousand suns, and I'm feeling pretty burned out as it is.

Walker blinks at the price, utterly unfazed. "That's not even remotely too much."

"Stop bragging," I grumble, dropping the price tag to cross my arms.

But that doesn't stop Walker from buying the dang thing because, as he says, "It's got the best online rating." Minutes later, he's loading it into his car.

I can tell he feels bad about the whole Saint thing, as relieved as he must be that I finally listened to him. When I told him it was over, he saw my red-rimmed eyes and wrapped me in a hug, asking no further questions. I couldn't help but appreciate that.

Later, when Walker is driving us back to the complex, he turns to me with a serious expression. Even more so than usual.

"You know I'm here for you, right? I'm on your team, Kin."

The persistent ache in my chest that began this morning subsides a little. Walker is here for the long haul. If anyone is going to look out for me and my kid, it'll be him.

"I know. Thanks, Walker."

And maybe it's selfish—short-sighted, even— but I can't help but wish that I could have just one more Boston Titan on my team. Specifically, the one with the sweet words and even sweeter kisses. But I know for all parties involved, it's better off this way.

For the baby, it has to be.

10

SAINT

Whoever invented running was a complete and utter sadist. Don't get me wrong—it's an excellent way to stay in shape during a long off-season. But at the same time . . . fuck this.

No, seriously. Fuck it.

After I sprint through the final stretch of my hour-long route, my worn Nikes slow to a regular walking pace at the park across the street from my building complex. I flop down on an empty bench to catch my breath, stretching my legs in front of me with a groan. I'm gonna feel this one for at least a week.

I pull my phone out of my running armband and pause the playlist, now on its second play-through. Not that I actually heard any of it. A morning run was meant to clear my head, but instead it just made it impossible to ignore my thoughts. Thoughts of Kinley, to no one's surprise, played on a constant loop.

It's like my brain is jammed in place, stuck on the expression on her soft face the last time we were in the same room together. She was so pale, as if all the warmth we'd shared the night before had been sucked right out of her. And then when she said we couldn't be together again . . . I don't know. It just didn't seem like her. She's usually so present, but this time she was a million miles away with a faraway, almost sad look in her normally bright eyes. A painful pinch had stabbed through my chest at her words.

My phone vibrates with an incoming text. It takes me a second to realize who the number belongs to, but when I do, I frown. It's the girl I was supposed to hook up with before I met Kinley.

Hey hottie. You up for any fun tonight?

Is it weird that I have zero interest in getting horizontal with some stranger? The old me would have jumped all over that. Now, though? I'm honestly just confused. All I want is for Kinley to talk to me and tell me where we stand.

A nagging sensation pulls at my gut. Is this really the end of us? I don't know if I can accept that. My phone stares back at me from where it sits in my hand like I'm supposed to know what to do about it.

This is so unlike me. I'm not a thinker . . . I'm a doer. So I need to *do* something.

With adrenaline and endorphins still flooding my veins, I pound out a message I'll probably regret later.

I'm at the park if you want to talk.

It's a simple invitation, one that I hope won't scare Kinley away more than I already have. I just need her to talk to me. I need her to trust me. Whatever the hell is going on, I know we can figure it out.

We've developed such an easy rapport, right from the moment we met. Surely, talking is what we need to do. Swapping sentences and words and truths with each other. And while these aren't sentiments I've felt, like ever, for a woman, I know it's what we need to do. Maybe then I'll stop obsessing like a heartbroken teenager.

Sighing, I drop my phone on my lap and lean my head back to stare at the treetops. This is probably pointless. She hasn't responded to any of my other texts recently, so why would she reply to this one?

I've been racking my brain trying to figure out what I did, where I went wrong. But for once in my life, I don't think I'm the problem. I'm willing to bet my left nut on the probability that it has something to do with Reeves.

Son of a bitch. Why did I have to fuck around with the sister of the dude who hates me the most?

But it isn't just "fucking around" to me. It's been a lot more than that. Hell, we haven't even had sex yet. Sure, we've made out on more than one occasion. I guess we swapped oral that one time. And I did finger-fuck Kinley to nirvana and back while she jerked me off the face of the earth.

Even though my heart rate responds by escalating to those very pleasant memories, my time with her wasn't about getting in her pants.

What I'm trying to say is that this hasn't just been about hooking up. We've been taking it slow in our own way, like we're building up to something important. And that's the thing. Kinley is important to me. I'm not sure what that means yet, but it's definitely not what the captain—

"Saint?"

Speak of the devil, and his angel of a little sister will appear.

I nearly give myself whiplash looking over my shoulder to see Kinley approaching, wearing a casual T-shirt that stretches tightly across her belly, and a ripped pair of jeans. I try not to stare as she sits down on the bench next to me.

"Hey," I say on a long exhale, so stupidly happy to see her again. What was I so worried about?

"Hey," she says, her voice guarded. Her hair is loose around her face, and she's wearing makeup. I don't recall if I've seen her wear makeup before. Her lips look even more kissable than normal, painted a soft pink color.

Stop staring at her mouth, I remind myself.

"Thanks for meeting me. How are you? How's the little man?" I tip my chin toward her belly, which appears to have gotten bigger in the few days since I've seen her, if that's even possible.

"I'm okay." She sighs on an exhale. "The little man is doing great. How are you?"

"I'm better now."

Rather than her usual easy grin, she's wearing a tight smile. She waits patiently for me to say something else, and it's in that precise moment that I realize I have nothing prepared.

Fuck. Time to wing it.

I rub one hand over my hair. "I'll just cut to the chase. I know your life is complicated right now. I mean, I can't fully understand it because I haven't walked in your shoes, but I get it. You've got a kid on the way and a brother to think about. I'm not trying to get in the way of your family or cause any drama. I just . . . I like hanging out with you. I want you in my life, Kin."

That seems to do something to her. What exactly, I'm not sure.

Her eyes close briefly before settling on mine again, and she lets out an uneasy sigh. "I'd like that. It's just that we can't—"

"See each other anymore," I say, repeating her words from before.

"Right. There just isn't room for it all."

I swallow my objections. So what if she doesn't want to fuck me? The woman has a lot on her plate right now with the baby landing in T-minus one month. Not to mention her very complicated family dynamics, meaning her brother is an asshole.

Man enough to handle a little rejection, I almost believe the words coming out of my mouth next. Almost. "We could be friends, you know—*just* friends. You gotta have room for one more friend in your life, right?"

"Are you . . . sure?"

"For once, yeah. But I don't want to pressure you into hanging out with me if you don't want to. It's your call. Take it or leave it."

She frowns. "What would that even look like?"

"What do normal, nonsexual friendships look like?"

Her eyes light up even as she scoffs, a little bit of that familiar humor sparking behind them. "Nothing like what we've been doing."

We share a look that has me thinking about *what we've been doing* in megawatt high definition. Fuck, these shorts are too damn thin to hide a chub.

Breathe, Saint. Do not think about her naked.

"Well, then we know what *not* to do." My voice is filled with humor, and Kinley surprises me by grinning.

"I've never been friends—just friends—with a guy before. What would we even do?"

"Well, you'd respond to my texts, for starters."

I elbow her in the arm gently, and she chuckles.

"Okay, I can do that. But no more suggestive emojis. And you'd have to stop doing that looky-loo thing with your eyes when you look at me."

"What eye thing?" I do the eye thing. It's an elevator eyes slash eyebrow-waggle combo that somehow always gets me laid at the club.

She elbows me back, *hard*.

Grinning, I lift my palms in the air. "Fine, fine. No looky-loo thing."

Her mouth lifts in a satisfied smile. "And no more late-night hangouts either," she says, glancing at my lips, and when I wet them with my tongue, she blinks and looks away.

"No late nights. Got it. Now that we've got some ground rules, what *would* you like to do together?"

She thinks for a minute, tapping her index finger to her chin. "We could . . . go to the farmers' market again, I guess."

I consider this, but it honestly feels underwhelming. "The farmers' market isn't until Saturday. Come on, let's christen our friendship by doing something *today*. Anything in the world you want to do, I'm game."

I know I'm being pushy as hell, but I can't help myself. I'm desperate to hang out with her. I've also been bored as fuck, trying to live on the straight and narrow path Coach has laid out for me. Sure, I could call up my boys and hit up a few clubs, but where would that get me?

"Anything?" She chews on her lip, staring far off across the street as she thinks. "Well, I've been dying to get a pedicure, but I don't really want to go all by myself. And since I haven't made any girlfriends here yet, you could go with me."

She meets my eyes, serving me a challenge like she's testing my commitment to the new parameters of our friendship.

I did say anything in the world, didn't I? This isn't exactly what I had in mind, but I'm nothing if not a man who delivers on his promises.

"Pedicures sound perfect."

Kinley blinks, clearly surprised. "Really?"

She's obviously underestimated me. I rarely say no to new things. Bungee jumping? Sure. Threesome with the couple I just met? Why not. Try the kangaroo tartare at a fancy steakhouse? You only live once.

"Yeah, really."

"Do you want to go now?" The excitement mounting in her voice is downright adorable.

"I'd better shower first. I don't want my smelly gym shoe feet to assault the nice, uh . . ."

"Nail technician."

"Right. Nail technician. Want to meet up in like thirty?"

Kinley nods, and her mouth lifts into a smile that I feel all the way inside my chest.

Maybe dialing back our physical relationship and keeping things platonic won't be so bad after all. Especially if that smile is still a part of it.

• • •

"This is heaven."

"Right?" Kinley presses her temple against the headrest so she can look at me, both of us blissed the fuck out. "This is my favorite part."

Our feet are submerged in large glass bowls filled with some steaming herbal mixture. It's doing wonders on the callouses on the back of my heels. I'm a little ashamed to admit that I've never done this before. I mean, I take care of myself, but my version of self-care usually involves fewer essential oils and more shots of tequila.

"I could get used to this," I murmur, sinking back into my chair.

"Mmm . . ."

A comfortable silence stretches between us that gradually feels less and less natural as we listen to the soft chatter of the other customers around us. This would be a perfect opportunity to fall back into our natural rhythm of conversation, but now that flirting is off the table, I'm coming up as blank as newly resurfaced ice.

Fuck, what do friends talk about?

"What's the rest of your week look like?" Kinley asks, expertly breaking the ice.

"Oh, you know. More of this. I'm gonna get a pedicure every day for the rest of my life."

She laughs from somewhere deep in her belly. "I've created a monster."

"You sure have. And I don't really have any plans. This morning, I got an invitation to my teammate Alex's bachelor party, but that isn't for another three weeks."

"Alex Braun?"

"The one and only." I quirk an eyebrow at her. "You've been researching the team?"

A faint blush rises on her cheeks. "I've been perusing some headlines. Alex is on a lot of them."

"I'm on more." The words come out on a sigh, distinctly *not* a brag.

"Not recently," she murmurs, her gaze flitting across my face.

Has she been researching me? I need a subject change before I start reading into shit that isn't there.

"How about you?" I ask. "Any grand plans?"

"Like I said, I don't really have any friends here. Besides you. And Walker."

I frown deeply at his name. "Yeah, you need more friends."

"I know."

"Why don't I introduce you to Aspen and Summer?"

"Who?"

"My teammates' ladies. Alex's fiancée and Tate's wife, respectively."

"You would do that?"

"Of course. You three would get along like a house on fire."

"Sounds dangerous."

"Only for me. They love talking shit."

Kinley gives me a smug smile. "Oh, then I'll definitely get along with them."

"Like I said."

There's a brief pause before Kinley releases a soft, happy sigh that makes goose bumps run up my arms. "Thank you, Saint."

"You're welcome."

Suddenly, she gasps, a hand flying up to touch her belly. "Whoa, big kick. Wanna feel?"

My mouth goes instantly dry. Of course I want to touch Kinley. But feeling her baby kick is just a reminder that she's got a whole life ahead of her that I don't have much of a place in.

Still, I slowly reach over and let her press my palm against the firm sphere of her belly.

Kinley's eyes sparkle with delight as she asks, "Do you feel that?"

Just that second, something flutters against my hand. A smile stretches across my face, mirroring hers.

"Yeah. I feel him. That's wild. He just does this all day?"

"Pretty much. He's gonna be a runner, I can already tell. I don't know how I'm going to keep up with him." She lowers her head to speak to her belly. "Mommy's gotta work in order to keep you happy and healthy, you know. She can't be chasing you all around New England."

I chuckle at the image of Kinley booking it after an itty-bitty toddler running at breakneck speed.

When do babies start crawling? Walking? I know so little about what it's going to be like for her once he's born. What kind of schedule will she have to follow? How much time will she have for herself? I wonder if she even knows yet.

"Kin, answer me this."

"Shoot."

"When you think about the future, what's the best-case scenario?"

"What do you mean?"

I scratch the side of my jaw with my free hand,

fully aware of the fact that my other hand is still resting on Kinley's belly, even though the baby settled at least a minute ago. "Are you still working? Are you a full-time mom? Do you want more kids?"

"Oh my God, is this twenty questions?"

"Yes, and I've got sixteen left, so you'd better start answering."

"Okay, okay." She laughs, then considers my question. "Hmm. In a perfect world, I'd still be able to work, probably part time. I mean, I care a lot about my career, and I don't think I'd want to give that up. Maybe I'll change my mind when I finally get to meet the little guy. I can't really know yet."

"Makes sense."

"As for other kids . . . I know it's crazy considering my situation, but yes, I want to have more. One more. A baby girl, hopefully. That way this guy can have a little sister to annoy him, and she can have a big brother to protect her."

"Kind of like you and Reeves?"

"Exactly. We don't have a perfect relationship, but in a lot of ways, Walker raised me when my mom was totally checked out, which was more often than not. I'm planning on doing a much better job than my mom ever did, but aren't we all trying to do better than our parents?"

"Eh, I don't think I could do much better than Cindy and Burt. I was their favorite."

"Um, aren't you an only child?"

I shrug, giving her a grin. "Yeah, so?"

Kinley rolls her eyes. "Classic only-child syndrome. So spoiled."

"Guilty. You aren't planning to spoil your kids?"

"Oh, absolutely not. I'm going to put this guy to work as soon as he figures out how to turn his own head."

We both laugh at that, her hand covering mine and giving it a squeeze. Friends definitely touch each other like this. At least, that's what I'm choosing to believe.

Eventually, she says, "I think he's done training for the marathon now."

It's a gentle reminder that my hand has overstayed its welcome, even as she traces small circles over the veins snaking over my knuckles.

"Right. Sorry." I pull back reluctantly.

"S'okay. That's the longest anyone else has felt him, I think, other than maybe the doctor. I'll bet he recognizes you when he gets here."

"Here?" I ask with wide eyes, twirling a finger around the salon. "Are you about to give birth on a nail technician?"

Kinley giggles and shakes her head, completely unaware of the fact that I'm using humor to deflect exactly how much that statement means to me. I didn't realize how badly I wanted to have a relationship with this kiddo until she said that.

"When he's older," I say, being serious for once in my goddamn life, "you can always drop him off at the rink. You know, if you have to focus on work. He can watch us play. I can even get him his own gear when he's big enough, and show him what's what on the ice."

Ducking her head, Kinley swallows hard and blinks rapidly.

Shit. Did I say something wrong?

But when she looks up at me again, she's glassy-eyed and her smile is radiant. "I'd love that."

A feeling of pride and loyalty and something else I can't quite name flows through me. All I know is that I'm going to do everything in my power to make Kinley's life better. Even if I'm "just" a friend, I want the absolute best for her and the kid. She's an incredible girl.

And she sure as hell deserves someone better than me.

11

KINLEY

Making friends as an adult is strange, to say the least.

Aspen texts me back just minutes after I send her a message introducing myself, and enthusiastically steers the conversation toward making dinner plans. Summer is a little slow to respond, but she does so with an apology about being in a session with a new client.

Soon, we've got a plan to meet up for an early dinner later in the day. I may be out of practice when it comes to new friendships, but that was easy enough, and I'm feeling surprisingly optimistic.

Truth be told, I'm a little nervous about this whole get-together. I have to make a good impression on them. As long as I'm in Boston, these women will be a part of my life in some shape or form. They're the significant others of my brother's teammates. Although, it was Saint who was thoughtful enough to make the introductions when I lamented the fact that I don't know any women in Boston.

A smile lifts my mouth when I think about the big, brawny Saint sitting next to me in the pedicure chair.

An hour later, I'm showered and dressed for my evening out, and I can't help but feel a little self-conscious about meeting new people. I try to tell myself that I have nothing to be ashamed of, but being single and *very* pregnant is an out-of-the-ordinary situation for a lot of people. I hope these women aren't the type to judge me.

I'll admit that another source of stress is that they sort of have local celebrity status because of the men they've bagged. Well, that's not entirely fair to them. Aspen has a high-up admin position for the team, and Summer is their licensed counselor, so both women are impressive in their own right.

Out of curiosity, I click through the tabloids surrounding the Alex/Aspen engagement and the Logan/Summer wedding, both searches yielding very limited information due to the private nature of both events. I do find ample pictures of Aspen and Summer, though, and holy *crap* are they both stunning.

To no one's surprise, they're even more beautiful in person.

Aspen smiles brightly at me from across the restaurant when I arrive, waving me over to the little booth where she and Summer are already seated, menus in hand. I suddenly feel like I've been invited to sit at the cool kids' table for the first time.

"You're so beautiful," Aspen exclaims, putting a friendly hand on my shoulder as I sit down.

"Oh, thank you." What do I say to that? What are words?

I feel more tongue-tied than I expected to. Maybe I'm just out of practice at this whole thing. I mean, sure, I keep in touch with my friends back home, but they're a thousand miles away.

Luckily, these women are natural conversationalists. It takes me a minute to match their energy, but by the time we've ordered our food, I'm smiling and laughing along with them.

Summer tells stories of Logan's brutish nature on the ice, and Aspen gossips about the single men on the team.

"Who have you met so far from the team?" Aspen asks through a mouthful of garlic bread. "Other than your brother, obviously."

"Um, just Saint. I met him when I first moved here because we all live in the same building."

"Walker and Saint live in the same building?" Summer shakes her head in disbelief. "Yikes."

Aspen nods, her already big eyes widening. "Doesn't that seem like a disaster in the making?"

"Why?" I ask, even though I already know the answer.

"Well, they treat each other with a lot of hostility," Summer says, her voice low. "Eden couldn't pay me a million dollars to try and mediate that conflict. I wouldn't even know where to start. Logan says there's no inciting incident behind all the tension. They're just 'different people,' whatever that means. They've never seen eye to eye on anything."

Is it really that bad? I didn't realize others were so aware of the strain between them. I guess neither of them are terribly subtle people.

I have more questions about Saint, but instead I find myself asking, "Who's Eden?"

"My boss," Aspen says with a proud smile. "She owns the team, even though she's our age. A queen among us. I'm sure you'll meet her soon."

"Wow," I murmur, feeling all the more out of the loop.

I guess I should have anticipated this. Summer is a full-blown hockey wife, and Aspen is soon to be. Being the formerly estranged sister of a hockey player and knowing virtually nothing about the sport or the dynamics around it puts me at a disadvantage.

The two women start chatting about the team, but I can hardly keep up with the name dropping. What I really want to talk about is Saint. I know how my brother feels about him—as if I could ever forget his disdain for the man—but I want a second opinion.

Aspen and Summer are on the inside, but also distanced enough to have an unbiased perspective on his character. Aspen sees him all the time because of his friendship with Alex, and Summer is a sports counselor, for crying out loud. If I want an educated opinion on Saint, I expect to look no further than these two.

". . . and Alex has Saint to thank for the tattoo on his ass."

That interesting string of words pulls me out of my thoughts. "What?"

Aspen rolls her eyes, but her ever-present smile grows. "When Alex and I first met, he made a dumb bet with Saint that he wouldn't fall in love with me." She wiggles her hand at me, the diamond on her finger almost as big as the almonds in my salad. "Obviously, he lost that bet."

"Gorgeous ring. What's the tattoo?"

"Guess."

"An emoji," I say with zero hesitation.

Aspen's eyes go wide. "Oh my God, how did you know? It's a heart-eyes emoji, fully colored."

"Heart eyes?" I gape, covering my mouth to stifle the laugh bubbling out of me. That sounds *exactly* like the Saint I know.

"Yep. I can't even be mad, since technically Saint was rooting for me before I even knew I liked Alex. It makes me laugh whenever I see it—without fail. Alex talks about getting it removed every other day, but I know deep down he likes it. It has meaning now. I can't believe you guessed right away."

Well, Saint and I have communicated with a lot of emojis since we met.

Both women give me a curious look, but I just smile, enjoying this story probably more than I should. The Saint she's talking about is very familiar to me—the one with a sharp sense of humor who can also appreciate a dumb joke. The bet doesn't surprise me at all. Saint is competitive, always looking for a game to win. That's what makes him so much fun.

"Saint's a good guy," I say, instantly realizing how dumb I sound.

Aspen and Summer blink at me, waiting for me to contribute a story of my own, but I've got nothing. Unless I start gabbing about one of our many steamy hookups, which I still remember in brilliant sound and color. I don't think the three of us are quite *that* close yet to swap intimate details.

"Um, I mean, he's been really helpful, what with me being pretty much useless at nearly eight months pregnant. He, uh, took me to the farmers' market. We just got pedicures yesterday." I somehow manage to stop rambling before completely going off the conversational deep end.

Aspen pauses, her fork halfway to her mouth. "Saint . . . got a pedicure?" Her tone is filled with disbelief.

I nod, clamping my mouth shut.

"That's sweet," Aspen says, recovering and nodding encouragingly.

God, I've become so socially inept in my solitary confinement. It's like my only skill now is being huge and making things awkward.

"That's *something*," Summer says, staring at me with something that feels a lot like suspicion.

Aspen jumps in again, reaching across the table to squeeze my hand. "You know, I'd be happy to help you out sometime. I used to babysit my little cousins."

She glances at Summer, giving her a look that prompts her to say, "Yeah, same. I'd be happy to help out. And we're much better friends than Saint."

"Do you two not like Saint?" I ask, forcing my voice to be as casual as possible.

"Saint is . . ." Aspen sighs and looks at Summer. "How should I put this?"

Summer shrugs. "I don't know him as well as you do."

"Well, let me preface this by saying that he's awesome. Total 'life of the party' kind of guy. And he can be a real sweetheart when he tries to be."

"But?" I brace myself, barely breathing.

A very big part of me doesn't want my brother

to be right about Saint. I want to know that I'm a good judge of character, that I can trust myself. If I can't trust my own instincts, what kind of mother will I possibly be?

Aspen shrugs. "He's kind of a wild card. I've known the man for years, and I'm still not really sure if I actually know him at all. He's really unpredictable, which is probably what makes him a great hockey player. But as for boyfriend material . . ." She makes a *so-so* gesture with her hand, tilting it from side to side.

Immediately, I go on the defensive. "No, that's not what I was—"

"Oh, I didn't mean to imply—"

"Yeah, we're not—"

"Totally. I shouldn't have—"

"That's okay. I'm sorry for interrupting you."

"No, no, *I'm* sorry for suggesting—" Aspen gives me an apologetic look.

Summer cuts in, graciously ending whatever the hell that painful back-and-forth was. "All that is to say we're here for you if you ever need a helping hand and don't feel like asking Boston's most unreliable."

I return their genuine smiles with a forced one of my own. "Thank you. That means a lot to me."

And it does. Even if I'm slightly crushed by the idea that Saint isn't the man I thought he was.

Later, when they hug me good-bye, I feel a sense of female kinship that I haven't felt since I moved to Boston. But when I watch them walk down the street to where their cars are parked, I can't help but think that it's all thanks to Saint. He's the one who offered to introduce us and put all this in motion. If not for his intervention, I'd be alone in my condo, probably eating cup-o-noodles for dinner and spiraling in my thoughts.

Boston's most unreliable.

I asked for their opinion of Saint, and I got it, although it's not the one I wanted to hear. What I wanted was for someone who knows him to reassure me that my feelings for him aren't completely irrational. That he's a good man.

Whoa. Do I have real feelings for Saint? The question presses on my heart with an answer so obvious that it feels silly to ask myself in the first place.

When the bus pulls up to the curb, I turn away, opting to walk back to the complex. I need time to think. To reset. Maybe to burn off a few of the calories from my fettucine alfredo.

By the third block, my feet are already sore, but the ache grounds me in the present.

Having a crush on your hot neighbor isn't the same as having feelings for him. I'm just finding something to obsess over, something to distract me from my impending reality. I'm going to be a single mother soon, and I probably won't have time to date again until my son is off at college.

Jesus. That's as surreal as it is depressing.

It takes nearly an hour, but when I finally make it home, I'm utterly exhausted. Having collapsed onto the couch and kicked off my shoes, then propped my sore feet on top of some pillows, I'm dozing off when my phone buzzes in my purse, a message from Saint waiting for me.

How's the rumor mill these days? ;-)

My chest compresses with guilt. I wonder if he has any idea how the people closest to him talk about him when he's not around.

I mean, Saint's clearly joking now, but he brought this up for a reason. He's plenty aware of the reputation he has from the tabloids. He must suspect that his friends have formed opinions on his behavior too. That hurts my heart to think about.

I know I promised him I'd return his messages, but I can't deal with this right now. I shove my phone back into my purse, losing myself in my thoughts before I drift off into a fitful sleep.

• • •

When I wake up from my nap a while later, my phone taunts me.

Blinking to clear my bleary eyes, I try to resist the temptation to internet stalk Saint, but that little devil on my shoulder wins out. I snatch up my phone and enter his name in the search bar, not surprised to see hundreds of results.

Wincing, I click on the first link and stare down at the internet article in disbelief as doubts swirl inside me. This right here has been what my brother has been trying to tell me. Saint is actually a sinner, it seems.

I clench my phone and let out a loud sigh. I don't want to read anything more about Saint's wild night, which allegedly ended in a threesome.

A threesome? Like, who even is this guy?

The Saint I'm falling for buys me prenatal vitamins and takes me to the farmers' market. He's flirty, sure, but he's been as wholesome as they come. A complete gentleman. He makes sure I'm fed and rubs my sore feet. He texts me for no reason, just to check on me.

Unless I've been duped, this isn't the man the world knows. They know the party boy who goes clubbing on a random weeknight and gets caught in compromising photos with women of every variety.

My heart throbs painfully and I draw in a slow breath.

I hate this, and I especially hate my brother being right about it. I hate that even *if* Saint has had some sudden desire to clean up his act, I'll never be enough for him. I'm not kinky or exciting or into threesomes. I'm about to be a *mom*. I like sex, of course, but it's all been fairly vanilla, and I'm certainly not a party girl.

Maybe that would have been fun when I was younger, but now I never will be. I'm entering a new season of my life, which includes responsibility and stability and making good decisions for my future. My future doesn't include hockey playboys. It can't.

I touch a hand to my belly, feeling a lump form in my throat as a knock sounds on my door. Walker has plans, so it can't be him, which leaves only one person. *Saint*.

Great. I guess I have to deal with this now.

I answer the door and let Saint inside. But he must sense my energy, because he lingers beside me in the entryway.

"What's wrong?"

I chew on my lip, looking for the right words to say. I wish I'd had time to rehearse them, to practice what I should say. Instead, it's like ripping off a Band-Aid.

"I'm sorry. I can't do this anymore." I gesture between us.

"Why? What happened?"

"This." I hand him my phone, which is still pulled up to the article.

He takes a quick glance, and his expression sours. "So, that's it then? You catch wind of my past, cast your judgment, and just bail?"

Suddenly uncomfortable, I shift from one sore foot to the other. "What? No, I . . ."

Saint has never once judged me or looked down on my past. And, *hello*, I clearly have one, including a baby daddy. My life was a little turbulent before Saint came into it.

"I'm not *judging* you," I say to clarify. "More like establishing some boundaries."

Saint raises his eyebrows. "Boundaries?"

I nod. "I've never had a threesome in my life, and I probably never will."

His lips tilt up. "And that's what you think I want because—"

"Because, um, because of that." I glare at the phone still in his hands.

"I've always been a *try anything once* kind of guy, Kin. Believe me, one woman is all I need."

Tilting my head, I weigh his words. I wish I could believe him, but part of me isn't sure. I don't know what to think anymore.

Saint hands me back my phone, then places a carton of shiny plums in my other hand. "I actually came by to bring you these. Just . . . let me know if you need anything."

My chest squeezes, and I swallow a lump in my throat. "Okay."

He turns to leave, and when the door closes behind him, I feel like curling into a ball and crying, and I don't even know why. Saint and I are friends, and I just pushed him away because of my own fears and insecurities.

Sometimes, I really hate these overactive pregnancy hormones. I have no idea if I made the right decision by confronting him, or if I just blew up the one good thing in my life.

● ● ●

The next morning, I'm heading out to go downstairs to check my mail, but am surprised to see a pink pastry box on the floor in front of my door. When I carry it inside and open it, I find it's another cake. This time, the loopy script on top of it reads, I'M REALLY, REALLY SORRY.

I can't help but laugh. The cake is beautiful with thick vanilla buttercream, and it smells like lemons. I inhale and then grab my phone to text Saint.

You're forgiven.

He replies a second later.

You sure? Just like that?

Yes. I'm the one who should be sorry. I shouldn't have judged your past.

It's all good. And for the record, three-somes aren't as fun as you'd think. So many elbows.

I roll my eyes. *Gross.* Before I can come up with a response, Saint texts again.

Sorry. Am I still forgiven?

I laugh because this conversation is ridiculous.

Yes. But stop sending me cake. I'm going to get fat.

You're perfect. Now go eat your cake. I'll talk to you later, okay? I'm going to the gym with the guys.

Okay. :)

12

SAINT

I'm not sure what I thought being "just friends" would look like, or what the hell I was thinking when I suggested it. All I know is that I'm a damn fool for slamming the friendship brakes on a relationship with a woman like Kinley.

Not that I had much choice in the matter. When it comes to having Kinley in my life or losing her for good, I'd make the same decision a thousand times over.

But that doesn't mean I'm not gonna pretend like this whole situation doesn't completely suck. If the tabloids were still up my ass like they were earlier this year, the top headline would read something humiliating like:

Defenseman FRIEND-ZONED by Captain's Sister—How Far Will He Bend Over Backward?

I'm as whipped as a guy can get without actually getting any ass. Exhibit A, I'm helping Kinley around the condo today, setting up the crib and painting the nursery walls. And since I never arrive empty-handed, I brought her favorite takeout.

Our new friendship boundaries are kind of strict now that we've agreed to no late-night romantic dinners, so a late-afternoon lunch standing around the kitchen island will have to do. It doesn't hurt that I scored her trademark floodlight smile in return, making all my inner turmoil seem worth it.

While Kinley rattles off her to-do list for today, I nod along and make mental notes to also help out in other ways not listed. Like putting new batteries in the lagging analog clock on her kitchen wall, and taking out the trash before I leave.

As much as I want to be the guy who jumps in bed with Kinley—which I do want very, very much—I'd rather be useful. I'm not just some dick-brained sleazeball who's only spending time with her to get in her pants.

I want to prove that to her. And to myself.

Speaking of pants, mine are uncomfortably tight at the most inopportune times. Looking at Kinley. Brushing fingers with Kinley. Smelling Kinley when the draft from the open window floats the scent of her fruity shampoo toward me, damn near assaulting my unsuspecting senses.

I'm doing my damnedest to focus on the platonic aspects of our relationship. The jokes, the teamwork, the casual conversation . . . things I could share with anyone. But with my dick half-hard and crammed up against my zipper at all times, the most innocent glance from her feels like she's stripping me naked with her eyes. Or maybe I'm the one stripping her naked with *my* eyes. Either way, sex is never very far from my brain.

And here's the thing—Kinley is undeniably pregnant. Since I met her, her belly has grown twice the size, from round bump to full-on cantaloupe. She looks like she could pop at any second. I know for a fact that would send most guys running for the hills.

But apparently, I'm not most guys.

To me, Kinley has never been more beautiful. She's gorgeous, if I'm being honest. Maybe that makes me some kind of freak with a pregnancy kink, but I'm more attracted to her than I've ever been. Her silky-soft skin and hair seem to emit their own UV rays.

And her breasts—*Christ*, her fucking tits—are heavy, swollen and brushed with a golden tan. I know from the reading I've done that they must be tender, in desperate need of soothing from careful hands. When I catch her giving herself a discreet comforting squeeze, I nearly drop the screwdriver I'm using and cream my goddamn pants.

All I can think about is screwing Kinley.

In the kitchen. Over the bathroom sink. On her bed. On the freaking nursery floor. We got so close before, and have even gotten each other off more than once. But I haven't been lucky enough to go all the way with her.

I want to erase any space between us. I want to bury myself deep inside her. I want to feel every inch of her, pushing all her buttons until she can't take it anymore, and finally, wildly comes on my—

"Oh, hey, that was quick."

I blink, returning to the present where I've somehow managed to put a whole crib together while thinking filthy thoughts. Which is obviously super creepy.

God, I really need to get it together.

I look up from where I'm crouching on the floor to see Kinley nodding approvingly at my work. When she rests a grateful hand on the back of my neck, a bolt of electricity spears straight from her palm to my dick.

Fuck, that almost hurts. Yeah, it's definitely been too long since I've had sex.

"This is perfect, Saint. Thank you. Wow, you're really warm. Are you feeling all right?"

"Yeah," I lie, feeling the opposite of all right. "It's just hot in here."

"I'll get you some water and turn on the A/C."

Kinley steps out of the room and I look for an escape route, half considering climbing out the nearest window. Is there any world in which I could bail without causing a scene? I could just tell her I'm going for a walk to clear my head, but then circle back to my place to jerk off. It would take me twenty minutes, tops. Or I could fake a phone call and—

"Oh, come on . . ."

When I hear Kinley fussing in the kitchen with the water filter, I think better of it. She needs me here. It would be classic Saint to bail, but the new and improved me isn't such a coward. So far.

With a little adjusting, I manage to get my semi under control before Kinley returns with two glasses of ice water.

She hands one to me. "Here you go."

I tip the glass to my mouth and chug, feeling less and less like an animal in heat every time the ice hits my teeth. When I finish, I wipe my lips with the back of my hand. "Thanks."

"Thank *you.*"

"All in a day's work. Hey, where did you want me to put those stencils of the hot air balloons? I was thinking the wall above the crib would . . ." I trail off when I see the far-off look on her face. "You okay?"

She blinks at me like she forgot I was there for a second. "Oh . . . I'm fine. Physically, for once."

"And mentally?"

She pauses, taking a swig of her own water before she responds. "I think it all just hit me."

"What did?"

"Everything. I'm about to have a child as a single parent. I have almost no one to rely on outside of you and Walker."

"Kin, neither of us are gonna let anything bad happen to—"

"I know, I know. I'm not ungrateful. I kind of feel the opposite. Unworthy."

When I try to object, she waves the thought away.

"It's just, what about when the season starts? Walker and I fell out of touch for a reason, you know. It was pretty much impossible to reach him. He was so busy. Understandably," she says quickly, rambling like she does when she's nervous, "since the stakes are so high in professional sports. But what am I going to do if I need help and neither of you are around?"

I gingerly place my hands on her shoulders and turn her until she's looking at me straight. "Hey, listen to me. It's gonna be okay. He and I may not see eye to eye on most things these days, but at least we agree on one thing. Taking care of you. There's no chance you'll ever be without at least one of us. I promise."

Skeptical, she tilts her head. "What about games? What about travel?"

Kinley has a point there. Unless Reeves gets his way and I'm officially suspended next season, we're both going to be out of town a lot. She has a right to be concerned.

Instead of trying to ease her worries with meaningless words, I tuck away all my instincts to just *make it better* and listen for once in my damn life.

"What do you need, Kin? I'll make it happen."

She looks at me like I don't know what I just offered. Little does she know, I'd do just about anything for her.

"Um, an entire team of professional caretakers would be great. And more baby clothes. And diapers. God, I'm gonna need so many diapers. Ugh, why am I crying?"

I wipe a stray tear from the soft ridge of her cheekbone. She leans into my touch, resting her head against my hand momentarily before sighing wetly. Dang, just the sight of her feeling so vulnerable has me tied up in knots.

Sniffing away her tears, she looks up at me and says softly, "I just need to know everything is going to be all right."

"It is. I promise you." An idea occurs to me, and I spout it out before it's fully formed. "One thing at a time. First, I'm going to throw you a baby shower."

"What? No, Saint, I don't know if I love that idea."

"Come on, what's not to love? Friends, family, themed snacks, dumb games . . . *gifts*."

"Gifts?" This grabs her interest.

"All the gifts. Diapers and baby clothes."

"I guess that's not such a bad idea. But who would you invite on such short notice? I have like zero friends here."

I shrug. "The team and their wives."

Kinley shakes her head. "I don't know. I wouldn't want anyone to feel pressured to buy me anything. Most of them don't even know me."

"That's not true. You know Aspen and Summer. And didn't you say they offered to help with baby stuff? They would love nothing more than to pick out the cutest onesie. Hell, we could make it a competition. Liven things up."

Frowning, she gives me an unconvinced shrug. "What about the guys? I don't know any of them."

"As one of them, I can assure you that they'd like nothing more than to have an excuse to sit around and drink beer for a few hours."

Kinley finally cracks a smile. "Fair enough. I guess I could help with—"

"Ah, ah, ah." Playfully, I waggle a finger at her. "Nope. I don't need your help. I've got this."

She arches an eyebrow. "You sure?"

I can't believe I didn't think of this before.

With Reeves and me traveling so often during the season, Kinley is going to need to build a community of people who can be there for her, help her out in a pinch. This is perfect.

"What, you don't have faith in me?"

She chews on this thought for a moment, her eyes softening.

"Of course I do," she murmurs, but almost as soon as the words leave her lips, she gives me a firm look. "Just don't do anything crazy, okay? No dumb diaper games. One tasteful game, tops."

"Copy that."

• • •

A little while before the gang is due to arrive, I finish tying a tangle of balloons on the front door of my condo with a flourish, turning to my friend Lydia with a smile. "What do you think?"

She looks up from where she's filling a cooler with bottles of craft beer, fixing me with an unimpressed glare from under her dyed-blue bangs. "Aren't balloons a choking hazard?"

"The baby isn't here yet. Hence the shower."

"Right. When's the main attraction getting here, anyway?" she asks, sliding a beer across the counter to me before she cracks open one of her own.

I check my watch. "About fifteen minutes."

Damn, time flies when you're hanging streamers.

I'm hosting the shower at my place so Kinley didn't have the added pressure of having to clean her condo, or deal with the aftermath of a party.

"This is my first baby shower," Alex says when he walks through the door, Aspen close on his heels.

I accept the six-pack of IPA he's holding and nod. "I can tell."

Aspen laughs and holds up two expertly wrapped baby gifts. "We brought these too."

Logan and Summer head in next.

"Want anything, Saint?" Logan asks, and I hold my beer up in response.

"You did such a good job decorating," Aspen says with a gasp that would offend me if I didn't know her so well. "You could have asked me for help, you know."

"Ah, it was no big deal. I had Lydia's help."

Lydia scoffs at the sound of her name. She's the owner of one of the bars I frequent and is an old friend from college.

Our relationship is pretty love-hate, based on how many times she's had me thrown out of her establishment. In all fairness, I can be a sloppy drunk, so I always come back the next morning to pay my tab and leave a big fat apology tip. On more than one occasion, I've bought her flowers to make up for starting a fight the night before.

I'm lucky that she had her first kid last year and knows the ins and outs of baby showers. I did have to drop a sizable chunk of cash in her palm to convince her to come and help me set up, but that's neither here nor there.

One by one, couple by couple, my condo fills up with familiar faces and voices. Lucien and Camille, Coach Wilder, even Les.

Eventually, the door swings open to reveal Reeves, looking as disapproving as ever. He holds the door open wide for Kinley, who steps over the threshold like there's a trip wire waiting to ignite the whole place.

Wearing a long, flowy summer dress that looks like a watercolor painting fucked a tropical bird, she's like some fertility goddess blessing us mere mortals with her ethereal presence. For a long moment, I just stare at her, because she really is beautiful.

I catch her eye and beckon her toward me, not missing how Reeves makes a beeline for the couches where the rest of the guys are lounging, instead of joining us. I almost appreciate the lack of subtlety.

"Hey," I say to Kinley with my most charming smirk. "You look incredible."

"Thanks," she says, a little wide-eyed and wondrous. "I feel like a whale. You hung streamers?"

"I did. C'mon."

I lead her toward the armchair in the living room. It's comfy as hell, proven by the fact that I had to kick Alex out of it not two minutes ago.

Kinley sinks into the chair as she sizes up all the bodies surrounding her—most of them big, burly male bodies. If I weren't one of them, I guess I'd be pretty intimidated too.

"Comfy?" I give her a gentle squeeze on the shoulder, which seems to snap her out of whatever reverie she was just in.

"Yeah, thank you." She smiles up at me. "I

can't believe you actually did all this. You must be exhausted."

"Me? Nah. We've barely gotten started. Can I get you some water? Seltzer? Juice?"

"Seltzer would be awesome."

"One seltzer coming right up."

I turn on my heel and nearly run smack into Aspen and Summer, who have obviously been lurking over my shoulder, waiting for an audience with Kinley.

"Is this guy bothering you?" Aspen asks playfully as Summer grins over her shoulder.

Kinley throws her head back and laughs.

Summer nudges me away. "Go on. Get."

"I'm gone, I'm gone." I chuckle as I make myself scarce. Those girls are something else.

When I come back with Kinley's drink, she's completely immersed in a conversation with Summer and Logan, her gaze darting between the two as she listens intently to what I'm sure is the story of how they met. It's a good story, from what I can remember, so I don't interrupt. I pass off her drink, and she shoots me a grateful look before focusing back on the conversation.

The door swings open again, and Eden waltzes into my condo like she owns it, with her husband, Holt, on her arm. This is the first time I've seen her since the suspension meeting, so when she flashes a genuine smile at me, I can barely believe it.

"Hey, Eden, thanks for coming. Holt."

Holt's handshake is a death grip, as usual. He gives me a short nod and turns to Eden, gesturing with a gift bag so large, it could hold a small child. "I'll put this with the other gifts."

Eden turns to me to answer the question I didn't ask. "It's brimming with athleisure loungewear and maternity robes. I figured everyone's getting stuff for the baby, so I took it upon myself to pamper the mother."

I give her an impressed chuckle. "How thoughtful of you. I didn't think you had it in you, boss."

Eden throws her head back with the laugh of a matriarch dealing with a dirty peasant. "Oh, Saint. I've barely thought about you at all lately, and believe me, that's a blessing for both of us. Good to see your face."

With that, she leaves me at the door and runway walks to Kinley, who's doing a great *deer caught in the headlights* impression. I thought I'd have to introduce her around, but I can barely keep up with everyone. I guess it's been a while since I was in a social setting like this.

Later, when Eden gets distracted by the promise of Lydia's fruity cocktails in the kitchen, I find an opening. I crouch down to Kinley's level, placing a hand on her knee before I remember that her brother is within swinging distance.

"How are you feeling? Need anything?"

"Honestly, I'm good." And from the looks of it, she is. She's all glowing and smiling, picking at a plate of grapes and party mix.

"Huh. You're kinda an extrovert, aren't you?"

She shrugs happily. "More than kinda. I love being around people."

"Me too."

I have the overwhelming urge to drop a kiss on her forehead when I stand, but instead, I catch Reeves's eye from where he sits with Lucien. He nods to me, and I think I'm meant to take that as an invitation to come talk to him.

Here goes nothing, I guess.

Lucien spots me approaching and practically leaps from the couch to return to Camille's side in the dining room, where she's chatting with Coach and Les.

No witnesses if shit gets murderous. Great.

"Hey, man, how's it going? Can I get you another drink?" I say as I approach Reeves, feeling on edge immediately. What do they say? Kill 'em with kindness.

His brows drawn together, he gestures around the room with a half-empty beer bottle as he grumbles, "This party turned out pretty nice. You did all this?"

He sounds so skeptical that I'm kind of annoyed. "More or less."

"And what do you get out of it?"

Is this a trick question? "It's not about me."

His narrowed eyes widen ever so slightly. "Well, thanks."

What? Did I just slip into some bizarro alternate reality where Reeves doesn't hate my guts unequivocally?

"Of course. Happy to help."

I almost say something about Kinley being worth the trouble, but I don't want to push my luck. I'd bet my life on the chance that he never wants to hear her name come from my mouth ever again.

The rest of the afternoon goes by without so much as a hitch. After one raucous game—only one game, as per Kinley's request—involving trivia about celebrity babies, the party dies down.

While Aspen trades a good-bye hug with Kinley by the door, Alex pulls me aside. "You'll tell me when the jig is up, right?"

"What the fuck are you talking about? Are you drunk?"

"Maybe. Aspen's driving. But really, all this for Reeves's sister? What are you up to?"

I sigh. I should have seen this one coming. My friends know a version of me that I'm trying hard to shed, the one with his fingers crossed behind his back while he tells pretty lies. The one who cares about himself, first and foremost.

"Would you believe me if I just said that I care about her?"

Alex blinks. "Yeah, I believe you."

Surprised, I blink back. That was unexpectedly easy. "Well, there you go."

Alex shakes his head with a knowing smile. "You're lucky I'm a better guy than you, or you'd have a tattoo on *your* ass by the start of the season. An eggplant emoji."

"All right, fuck off." I chuckle, spinning him toward the door. He's of course referring to a bet I made with him where he lost and had to get a tattoo on his ass.

One by one, the guests depart, most of whom I'm sure will be continuing the party elsewhere. Normally, I'd join them, but not tonight.

"I asked Lydia if she needed any help in the kitchen, but she pretty much slammed the door on me," Kinley mumbles. "If your kitchen had a door."

"Yeah, she's a treat, that one. C'mon, I'll help you carry all the gifts to your place."

It takes us four trips, but soon enough Kinley's trove of treasures is piled high in her living room and it's time to say good night.

She walks me to the door slowly. Reluctantly, if I were reading into it. "Can I help you clean up your place?"

"Nah, Lydia's gonna stick around for a while and help. Thanks, though."

"Lydia," Kinley murmurs under her breath.

"She's a good friend. Seemed like you made a lot of friends yourself tonight."

"Yeah," Kinley says with a content sigh. "I got Camille's number."

"It'll be good to have another mom on call."

"Exactly." She pauses at the door, her hand on the knob. "Thank you for tonight. For everything."

A familiar feeling I can't quite name blooms in my chest. "Anytime."

"I mean it, Saint." Her expression is soft, and her eyes linger on mine.

"I mean it too."

We stand there for what feels like a lifetime, like we're trying to memorize each other's faces. And with how often Kinley's gaze drops to my lips, I think she wants me to kiss her. Or maybe I just want to kiss her.

Fuck, there I go again. Projecting my own desires.

Not wanting to misread the situation any more than I already have, I just crack an easy smile. "Good night, Kinley."

She blinks, her expression unreadable. "Good night. I'll text you."

"You'd better."

I step back into the hall and stand outside her door for a solid minute, wondering if Kinley is still lingering on her side.

Does she still want me? Does she really see me as just a friend? I don't know what to think anymore.

All I know is that I gotta get my imagination under control before it gets the better of me again.

13

KINLEY

She's a good friend.

Saint's comment about his "friend" Lydia is knocking around in my head like a dang pinball, interrupting my nighttime routine. It threw me because he's never talked about her before.

Is she new in his life? Are they seeing each other?

After removing my makeup with a cleansing wipe, I splash cold water on my face in an effort to knock some sense into my head. If they are seeing each other, he would definitely tell me. Right? We're friends. Friends tell each other stuff like that.

But at the same time, Saint and I aren't really *just* friends, are we? I mean, I guess we could qualify as friends with benefits. Or we did.

Maybe he doesn't want to tell me about the new girl in his life because he thinks it could be awkward for me. Or maybe they've been seeing each other this whole time, even while he and I were hooking up.

Oh God, that's the worst thought ever. But my brother was pretty insistent that Saint is bad news, so . . .

I'll bet they're tangled up in each other on his kitchen island right now. He's probably got his hands in her blue hair, and she's got her red lips on his perfect neck, leaving her mark on him. Imagining Saint's impressively sized erection being used for Lydia's pleasure. My heart throbs painfully.

I brush my teeth harder than usual, as if I could scrub my thoughts clean with toothpaste. I'm the one who nipped our "benefits" in the bud, so I have absolutely no right to be spiteful now.

Saint can fuck whoever he damn well pleases. I don't get an opinion.

Even as I tell myself this, I feel the jealousy reaching a boiling point deep inside me. In bed, I throw the covers over my head and hope these intrusive thoughts don't infiltrate my dreams.

But behind my eyelids, all I can see is his face disappearing behind a closed door, over and over on an endless loop.

I wanted him to kiss me before he left. Maybe that's selfish, but it's true. He didn't pick up on any of my cues.

What did I expect, for Saint to still be hopelessly into me? I can't fault him for moving on when I'm the one who asked him to. He's already doing enough for me as it is. He doesn't owe me anything. Throwing me that baby shower today was already so extra.

Suddenly overheated, I throw the covers off with a huff. I don't need to fall asleep to be trapped in a nightmare. If I continue to be so selfish, I may very well lose Saint for good.

Staring up into the darkness of my ceiling, I can't imagine anything worse.

• • •

"*This* is your place? Oh my gosh, Kinley. You're really moving up in the world."

My cousin Martha does a slow three-sixty as she takes in my condo, her little twin boys mimicking her by spinning in rapid circles. They're three years old with grinning mouthfuls of lopsid-ed teeth, and use big-boy words like *actually* and *Lamborghini*. The sight of their silly antics makes me break into a fit of giggles along with them.

The day after my baby shower, Martha reached out to me, asking if she and the kids could visit on their way to meet up with her husband. He's in New York on business for several days, and since they hadn't taken a family vacation together in over a year, they decided to kill two birds with one stone.

I wasn't sure how I would handle hosting a small family at thirty-eight weeks pregnant, but I'm honestly glad they're here. Keeps my mind off how crappy I feel.

"Here, let me take your bags," I say, reaching out.

Martha shakes her head vehemently. "Woman, you are pregnant. Haven't you learned? No manual labor. Guest room over there?"

She nods down the hall, and I let her find her way, the twins trailing behind her. The front door is still open, so I move to close it, but pause when I see a familiar face down the hall.

Saint stands at his door in his running gear, flip-ping through his mail. *Oofta*. Something about a man fresh off a long workout does it for me. His athletic shorts hang low on his hips and his T-shirt is damp with sweat, making it cling to all his muscles.

My heart hammers, and my hands itch at my sides, wanting so badly to touch him.

It's been two weeks since I saw him last, the longest we've gone without seeing each other since we first met. Sure, we've exchanged a text or two, checking in with each other. But seeing him in the flesh, all glistening and glowing, is an entirely different experience. He's unbelievably gorgeous. And I'm humongous.

Ugh.

"Saint," I call out, my voice catching in my throat.

Jeez, calm down, psycho.

He turns, popping out an earbud and flashing that killer smile at me. "Hey, stranger. You look well. How've you been?"

"Good," I say, leaning against the door frame as casually as I can. "My cousin and her kiddos are here for the night."

"Oh shit, another Reeves. How many of you are there?"

"Pretty much just her. Do you want to come by for a bit? I've got some lemonade on ice if you're thirsty."

Subtle much? I hope it's only obvious to me that I'm the thirsty one, and not for the lemonade. But the guy is a freaking thirst trap. I mean, *look* at him.

Saint doesn't hesitate for a moment. "That sounds perfect. I probably smell, though."

"I don't care," I say, and I really don't.

I hold the door open wide, and when he passes me, all I smell is that masculine musk I've come to crave. The pulsing of my heart is decidedly elsewhere now, warming the touch-starved territory between my legs. I need to cool down. Maybe I do need some of that lemonade after all.

Inside, Martha has reemerged from the guest room, holding her kids' hands.

"Who's this handsome young man?" she asks, doing her best impression of Grandma Reeves, even though my cousin is only a few years older than we are.

The older twin, Liam, immediately repeats, "Handsome," followed by Beck, the younger.

Martha and her husband are *big* alt-rock fans.

"This is Saint, my neighbor. He's on the same team as Walker."

"Wow, you're just crawling with beefcake here in Boston, aren't you? How long have you played hockey, Saint?"

Grinning good-naturedly, he says, "Oh, you know, just about forever."

Saint takes it from there, entertaining Martha and the kids while I pour us all glasses of lemonade. I watch from the kitchen as Saint kneels down to the twins' level, snagging a high five from each of them. Their hands look so tiny compared to his.

"Wet," Beck says, pointing at Saint's damp hair.

"Yeah, I'm a bit sweaty. I went for a run today. Do you two like running?"

"Yeah," Liam chimes in, pulling on his mom's hand.

"Why don't you show me?" Saint asks, more to Martha than the kids.

Smart.

"Don't knock anything over," Martha warns before letting them both go.

Liam toddles down the hall to the living room

and takes a lap around the coffee table, squealing with delight as Beck chases after him.

"Run, Saint," they call out, prompting Saint to follow after them in a slow-motion sprint.

The kids love this and dissolve into giggles, wrapping themselves around Saint's legs and sitting on his shoes so that he can "dinosaur walk" them around the condo. *Holy cuteness, Batman.*

My chest feels tight as I watch them. *Stupid pregnancy hormones.*

Martha shoots me an impressed smile as she helps me carry the refreshments. "He seems like a catch. Anything happening between you two?"

I shake my head with a sigh. "Unfortunately not."

Wait, *what did I just say?* I'm so thrown by my own subconscious making herself known that I nearly spill the tray of chips and dip I'm carrying.

Saint would be a great dad, obviously. But a dad to *my* child? I didn't let myself entertain that thought until right now.

Is that what I want?

No, that's crazy. I have a bad case of pregnancy brain. My hormones are in full swing right now.

That's all. Just because I have a bun in the oven doesn't mean every male I encounter is hungry for fatherhood.

Gross. Do better, Kinley. He's not my boyfriend. He's not gonna be a father-figure to my kid. Period.

While I silently scold myself, Martha tells a story about her pregnancy with the twins.

I should really listen since I'm due within the month, but I can't help but be distracted by the beautiful, burly man in the room. I watch Saint take long gulps of lemonade, his Adam's apple bobbing enticingly in his throat.

I don't see any hickeys . . . maybe he and Lydia aren't actually hooking up. Maybe that was just my imagination.

God, I hope so, but I don't know for sure. I guess I'll keep living with these little heart pangs and try to ignore how much they feel like regret.

14

SAINT

My head has been spinning constantly with thoughts of Kinley.

She's a great girl and I like her, more than I probably should, but there's a lot of complications that have been nagging at me. First, she's Reeves's sister, which *is* a problem. The guy hates me, and this would only make our team dynamic worse. And considering I'm already on thin ice, I need to tread carefully.

Second, there's no denying the fact that she's pregnant. It hasn't bothered me at all, which is maybe strange in and of itself. And as naive as I've been about the whole pregnancy thing, I know Kinley becoming a mom will change our relationship. Her focus will be on her child, and rightly so.

And do I even know how to take on a fatherly

role? Highly doubtful. I haven't ever been around a baby. Never even had a younger sibling. I wouldn't know the first thing to do, or how to support Kinley through all that, even if we were dating.

Which we're not.

These are the thoughts that replay on a constant loop. All day, I've tried to distract myself by doing different things to try to clear my head that usually work—like hitting the gym hard for some extra reps. I've also done my laundry and watched a UFC fight that I've been excited about, but I still can't get out of my own damn head.

Which is why when my buddy Alex texts me, I talk him into meeting me for a beer. Alex is in a serious relationship. Maybe he'll have some good advice for me.

• • •

"No way," Alex says, shaking his head when we sit down at the bar thirty minutes later.

"Just hear me out," I say, sliding the pint glass the bartender sets down in front of me toward Alex. I can tell based on the dark color that this is his oatmeal stout. This brewery opened last year, and it's quickly become a favorite of ours. Not that I've been out much lately.

Alex is still scowling at me as I wait for the bartender to pour my ale. I take a fortifying sip before continuing.

"I click with her better than any other girl. That has to mean something, doesn't it?"

He considers this and takes a drink of his beer. "Maybe." Then he scowls at me again. "But not necessarily. You also once tried to tell me that you felt something special with those redheaded twins." He wiggles his eyebrows at me.

I blush a little. Okay, the old Saint was a bit of a jackass. I'm not necessarily proud of how I acted in the past. Gotta love it when your buddy points out to you what an idiot you've been.

"That was a long time ago," I grumble.

Alex chuckles. "That was literally last summer, dude."

I roll my eyes. "Then please, by all means, impart some of your wisdom, my wise friend."

Alex exhales slowly, considering his words. "You know I say this with all love and respect, but what are you even doing? Not only is she Reeves's sister, but she's about to have a damn kid."

These are two facts I'm well aware of. "I know, man. I know, okay."

"Well, knowing it and living it are two very different things. Are you ready for that? A kid is a huge responsibility. And babies? A newborn?" He shakes his head and his eyes widen. "It's like no sleep and constant supervision. My nephew had colic when he was born, and it was awful for my sister. For months and months."

I can't imagine losing sleep for months, and then having to train and perform at the level I do during the day. That would suck . . . Alex is right about that. A sinking feeling twists in my gut.

"Hey, forget it, all right? Let's just enjoy our beers."

He nods and tips his chin at me. "You got it, buddy."

15

SAINT

Alex's bachelor party is at a bar in downtown Boston famous for its brisket sandwiches.

Being the little food nerd he is, and being too Type A to appoint a best man to handle the planning, Alex set it all up himself. We're a few appetizers deep now, clearing room for our entrees by stacking emptied pint glasses tall enough to make the waitress nervous.

When I return to the table after helping her carry the evidence of our team's insane tolerance back to the bar, Alex fixes me with a skeptical look.

"You flirt with her?"

"No," I say with a shrug. I guess she's cute, but the thought didn't even cross my mind. Honestly.

"Who are you and what have you done with my

best friend?" Alex growls, and the other guys join in on the ribbing just because they can.

"Our playboy is reformed. Now he's only got eyes for Reeves's sister," Logan says with a smirk, and I sock him in the shoulder.

"Shut the fuck up, Tate."

Reeves stands up from the table, muttering something about needing to use the bathroom. The man won't even look at me.

Five minutes ago, I tried to ask him what he was drinking, and he guzzled the whole thing down rather than respond to me. Message received, loud and clear. I thought we'd had a breakthrough at the baby shower, but apparently I'm still a jackass in his eyes.

It doesn't help now that the guys are giving me shit about having a crush on Kinley. The worst part is that they're totally right.

I sneak a glance at my phone, hoping to see a text from her. No luck. Aspen and the other women are a few blocks away at a wine bar, much classier than this joint. Kinley is there with them, probably serving as the chaperone since she obviously can't drink. I hope she's having fun at least. I sure as hell am not.

"Come on, man," Alex drawls, obviously on the slippery side of tipsy. "Give us the deets."

"I'll admit I'm curious too," Lucien mumbles through a mouthful of fried pickles.

"There aren't any 'deets' to share."

Tate rolls his eyes at me. "C'mon, man. Reeves is taking a shit. You can tell us."

Gross.

"What is this," I deadpan, "a scene from *Grease*?"

The musical reference goes catapulting over their heads. *Uncultured swine.*

"All right, if you really want to know, listen up." I lean in conspiratorially. The guys lean in too, looks of interest plastered on their dumb faces. For my own personal shits and giggles, I try to draw it out for as long as possible. "The thing about Kinley and me, you see, is that we . . . are . . . *friends.*"

They all groan in unison, throwing their hands in the air and settling back into their seats.

Alex scoffs. "Whatever, man. Let it be known that whatever is going on between the two of you, I saw it coming from a mile away. You heard it here first, folks."

"Hear, hear," Lucien says, raising his glass.

A second later, they're all toasting to a nonexistent relationship. Ain't that the saddest shit you've ever heard of?

"Yo, Lucien," Alex says suddenly. "What's it like being with a pregnant woman?"

Lucien shrugs, a devilish smirk stretching across his face. "A woman is a woman. The sex is great. Don't you agree, Saint?"

Fuck this. I'm equal parts intrigued and envious, so I keep my mouth shut and will continue to do so as long as we're on this subject.

I'm trying to keep the drinking to a minimum tonight in case Kinley needs me for some reason, but now I've got all sorts of dirty ideas in my head of what exactly she might "need" from me. If they keep this shit up, I'm about ready to chug what's left of this beer and order two more.

Reeves returns to a table of grown men giggling like a bunch of schoolgirls. Suspicious, he pins me with a glare. "What did I miss?"

"Nothing." I straight-up lie to his face, inspiring giggles anew from the peanut gallery.

Reeves cranks up the disdain by pushing past me to get to his seat. So much for that breakthrough, huh?

> 1. I sincerely hope Kinley is having a better night than I am, because this is bullshit.

16

KINLEY

"**W**hat do we think? Red or white to start with?" Aspen asks no one in particular, perusing the wine menu in the cozy booth we're all squeezed into together.

"I prefer white," Summer says.

Camille nods amiably. "Whatever you want, Aspen."

The bride-to-be turns to me and cocks her head to the side. "Do you have a favorite?"

"I alternate between the two, but it's up to you. I can't drink anyway." I pat my oversized belly with as much humor as I can muster.

Since we're sitting in a booth, I had to position myself at the end and point my torso to the side so my small planet of a body can fit without the table shoving into my belly. Long story short, I'm huge.

"Oh my God, I'm sorry. I'm such a dumbass," Aspen says, so genuinely contrite that I actually feel bad for her.

"Happens all the time when you're pregnant, right?" Camille cuts in, shooting me a look that says *I get you.* I appreciate this woman more than she probably knows.

"Right. Don't worry about it. I'll be just fine." I tap the menu's section labeled **MOCKTAILS** with one finger. "They've got some alcohol-free options I'm eyeing."

Aspen gives me a relieved smile. "Okay, good. I'm really glad you could come. I know it was kind of a last-minute invitation."

One week's notice was plenty of time for me, but I wouldn't dare admit that. These women seem to think I have a bustling social life outside of them, when in reality *this* is my entire social life. "Not at all. I'm so happy to be here."

The waiter comes and takes our orders, and it's just my luck that they're out of the alcohol-free seltzer I wanted to try. Aspen looks like she's about to fight the waiter for taking away my only shot at happiness this evening, so I just ask for some water and a glass of cranberry juice that I don't really want.

God, I miss wine so freaking much.

"Tell me about how you and Alex got together," I ask Aspen, doing my best to veer the subject away from my personal pity party. "I've only really heard about the tattoo bet with Saint."

The glances I get after mentioning Saint's name aren't lost on me. I'm sure these women have a lot of ideas about what's going on between the two of us.

If I'm being completely honest with myself, I kind of like the idea of others thinking that we're together. It's flattering. I like living in this fantasy where I never friend-zoned Saint for the sake of my brother's comfort. Can I justifiably blame Walker for all my heartache? If it weren't for him—

No, I'm not going there.

With a little encouragement from Summer and Camille, Aspen dives into the story of how the two of them fell in love, dropping in the surprise twist that Alex and Eden were once an item.

Wait, what? I had no idea.

"That's wild," I sputter, honestly shocked.

Eden doesn't seem like the kind of woman who would have patience for a man like Alex. That's probably why they aren't together anymore. Alex seems so playful and mischievous, and Eden is a buttoned-up professional. I don't see them together at all.

"It was all thanks to Saint, really. Has he told you about the cabin he owns up in Canada?"

A little dumbfounded, I blink. "No, he never told me."

"Well, I had nowhere to go after my ex kicked me to the curb, so Saint offered to let me stay there for the summer. Keep things in order, you know? Alex was up there doing some work around the property for him too, and . . . I guess the rest is history."

I smile and give her a small round of applause for the story, but my thoughts are elsewhere.

I guess there's a lot about Saint I don't know. I've only known him for six weeks or so. The thought that there's so much more to the man than I realized is both exciting and daunting. Exciting, because I want to know everything about him. Daunting, because I'm worried my feelings for him will grow the more I learn.

I miss him. Is he as miserable as I am right

now?

I'm surrounded by intelligent and compassionate female friends, and all I can do is pine for a man who will never be mine. I'm pretty much the worst.

After a couple of rounds of drinks for the table, I finally cave and obey the voice in my head begging me to just *go home*. I tell the others that I'm tired and my feet hurt—both very true statements—and they give me hugs and promises of more get-togethers to come.

"Thanks again for inviting me," I say into Aspen's ear as she hugs me tightly.

"Thanks again for coming. Go get some rest, okay?"

I wish it were as easy as that. The Uber ride back to the complex is quick and painless, but I still feel uneasy and weirdly wired now that I'm alone with my own thoughts.

Stepping out of the elevator, I glance down the hall at Saint's door. Before I can psych myself out, I hobble on my swollen feet until I reach his welcome mat. I knock, but there's no answer.

"Still out partying, huh?" I say to the peephole, almost expecting a response.

He must not be missing me as much as I'm

missing him if he's still out on the town. *Lucky guy.*

I sulk back to my condo and shut the door behind me with a hollow click, peering down at my belly with a heavy sigh. "Just you and me again, kid."

17

KINLEY

I wake with a startled gasp, realizing that my sleep shorts are soaking wet. Trying to get my bearings, I take in my surroundings.

Sunlight streams brightly through the window and across my bed, and I blink my eyes against it. I push myself upright and reach out with a shaking hand to confirm that my sheets are absolutely soaked. There's also an achy feeling in my lower back and pelvis. My water must have broken while I was sleeping.

Whoa. Okay then. I guess this is happening. I need to get to the hospital.

I grab my phone and call my brother. His phone rings for what feels like eons before I hear his voice.

"This is Walker, leave a message."

Ugh. The idiot probably drank too much at Alex's bachelor party last night and is still sleeping it off. I try three more times before I give up and call Saint.

He picks up after only two rings. "Hey, you okay?"

I sigh in relief, immediately calmed by his deep, warm voice that wraps around me like a comforting hug. "My water just broke. Can you come?"

Saint inhales sharply. "Yeah. On my way."

He makes it to my place in record time, probably three minutes or less. It's enough time for another achy feeling to grip my stomach down low. This is what contractions feel like, I'm guessing.

When I let him in, his hands fly up to my face, smoothing my hair into place and gazing down at me in concern.

"Are you okay?"

"Yeah, I think so. Thanks for coming."

"Of course. Have you had a—"

"Contraction? Yes, a couple minutes ago. Can you grab the—"

"Hospital bag? Closet, right?"

While I slump against the side of a chair, Saint rushes past me and grabs the duffel he helped me pack a few weeks ago—complete with a robe, a few fresh changes of clothes, a bag of toiletries, and a bag filled with baby clothes and necessities. Oh, and a phone charger with an extra-long cord, of course.

My second contraction hits me in the parking garage. This one is longer and even more intense than the first.

I groan against the pain, leaning my full weight against Saint, who holds me up like I'm just some cotton blowing in the wind. Meanwhile, I feel like there's an entire planet's worth of gravity dragging me down.

"Take a deep breath. I've got you," he says, his deep voice rumbling pleasantly as he just holds me in the middle of the parking garage.

I think I'd be more panicked if he weren't here with me. But in Saint's arms, I feel safe. Secure. Even if things are about to spiral out of our control.

I'm not sure how many contractions hit me before we make it to the hospital and I'm tucked into a bed. Five? Six? As the nurses prep me, I hold Saint's hand with the grip of someone hanging off a cliff's edge.

"Am I hurting you?" I ask him.

He shakes his head and presses soft kisses to my white knuckles. "Not at all."

"This is awful." I scrunch up my face, tears of pain leaking from the corners of my eyes and sliding down my cheeks. I feel delirious, like a scared little kid.

"I know, baby," Saint murmurs. "You're gonna get through it. Just breathe with me."

He takes a breath, and I stare into his eyes as I follow his lead. We breathe together. In and out. Together, we breathe through the next contraction and every one that follows.

Saint stands beside me when I get my epidural, and waits for hours with me in the little hospital room. When his stomach rumbles, I kick him out to go get some breakfast in the hospital cafeteria. He walks back into my room not half an hour later, and the doctor says it's time.

Together, we breathe through the doctor's commands to *push, push, push*. We breathe through every second, on and on for what feels like hours until a tiny, shrill cry signals the very first breath of my healthy, newborn baby.

I have a son.

. . .

"You sure he's safe back there?" Walker asks as he turns the key in the ignition.

We both glance into the rearview mirror to quadruple-check on little Caleb. He's sound asleep, safely bundled away in the car seat. I thought about riding back there with him, but I don't want to seem like a crazy lady. It's only a few minutes' drive back to the condo.

"Seems like," I say, gazing at my son's sweet face.

He's so perfect and tiny. Though, he sure didn't feel tiny coming out of my . . . unmentionables. Walker checked his voice mails after sleeping late, and made it to the hospital about an hour after Caleb was born.

"What else can I do for you today?" my brother asks.

He's been bending over backward, trying to make up for sleeping through my phone calls when I was going into labor. I've told him over and over again that it's okay, everything worked out just fine. But despite my reassurances, he's still pretty remorseful.

Or maybe he's just not pleased knowing it was Saint who was by my side through it all.

After my brother arrived at the hospital, Saint stayed just until he knew the baby and I were fine, and then he left, saying he wanted to give us some time as a family. I didn't want him to go, but I couldn't exactly make him stay either.

That was two days ago. Saint has texted me several times, and I've sent him an obnoxious number of pictures of Caleb sleeping.

"Walker, you've done enough. Really. Fielding friends and family and making sure I'm eating were my two big concerns. You've been a big help. Thank you."

"I can order you dinner tonight if that would—"

"That's not necessary. Saint's ordering us a pizza later."

Walker's fist clenches and unclenches against the steering wheel, and I brace myself for whatever he's going to say next.

It's no surprise that he doesn't approve of my evening plans with his least favorite teammate. But what ground does he have to stand on? Saint was the one who stepped in without a moment's hesitation when Walker dropped the ball. Or the puck?

Whatever. I'm a tired mama running on power naps and sheer willpower. I'm allowed to mix sports metaphors.

When Walker remains silent, I try again. "You can stay, you know. For some pizza."

"I've got a meeting with my agent later. Thanks, though."

Okay, so maybe he hasn't completely come around to the idea of Saint being a fixture in my life, but at least he's not vehemently opposed to it anymore. Pressing him any further on the subject would push my luck on them reconciling their differences. Better to let sleeping dogs lie.

By the grace of some higher power, Caleb snoozes all the way back to my condo. That "home sweet home" sensation has never really occurred to me here in Boston until this very moment.

Good-bye, weird hospital smells, and hello, familiar comfort. It's so nice to be home. Once I've removed Caleb from his infant carrier and placed him into his new portable bassinet in the living room, I sink into the couch.

There's a quick knock on the door.

Walker opens it, but not before visibly bracing himself. "Saint," he says, his voice stiff.

"Hey, Reeves. Good to see you. Congrats on becoming an uncle."

There's something so unnatural in how they talk to each other, even after all this time, but I have to appreciate the effort. I know it's for my sake. I can barely see Saint through the doorway with Walker blocking the way, but some shuffling suggests that they're shaking hands.

Progress.

"Thank you. And thanks for your . . . help. With Kinley."

I peer around Walker's back and shoot Saint a wide-eyed look as if to say, *I guess he's trying?*

Saint gives us both that trademark lopsided grin. "Happy to help."

I know my brother well enough to know he's wondering about Saint's time with me in the hospital . . . and if he saw anything he shouldn't have.

Gross.

When an attractive man who is definitely not your significant other assists you in childbirth, you make sure he doesn't see your lady parts. Trust me. I had a very strict *nothing below the knees* policy when it came to what Saint was allowed to see. Still, I can tell how squeamish my brother is.

It would be almost laughable if things weren't so tense right now.

"All right, Walker, let the man inside," I grumble at my brother.

Walker mutters under his breath, something about how he was *getting to that*, but he ultimately beckons Saint inside before leaning against the door frame himself.

"You staying for pizza, Reeves? I'm about to put an order in." Saint taps his phone screen and holds it up to his ear, presumably having saved a local pizzeria's number on speed dial. I don't know why that's so hot . . . it just is.

"I've got a meeting, but you two enjoy. Call me if you need anything."

While Saint's on the phone, I pull Walker in for a hug and squeeze him tight. "See? He's not so bad."

"*Not so bad* doesn't mean *good*, Kinley." Walker sighs, but I can see a trace of a smile lurking. He reaches out to brush what little hair Caleb has with his fingertips and whispers good-bye for now.

Watching my big brother fall so naturally into the role of sweet, attentive uncle fills my heart with a profound sense of pride. But I know Caleb's presence here is going to make my brother even more protective of me. Of us.

When the door closes behind Walker, it's Saint's turn to dote on Caleb. He walks over to where the baby is resting and reaches out to touch his belly with an adoring smile on his face.

"You made this," he says to me, then stares at Caleb's tiny sleeping face. The tone of his voice is boyish and filled with wonder.

I cozy up next to Saint, and he wraps his arm around my shoulders. I lean against his side, happy to have him here.

"Couldn't have done it without you," I say, nudging him.

Saint doesn't spare it a second thought. "*Psh*, you absolutely could have. I was just there to mop the sweat off your forehead."

"A vital part of the process."

"If you say so," he says, leaning in to drop a casual kiss on the crown of my head.

We both freeze, and I know—I just *know*—that we're wondering the same thing.

Are we really just friends? After everything?

I almost consider broaching the subject until a

giant yawn interrupts me. Saint squeezes my shoulder comfortingly, and I lean into the touch.

"You must be exhausted. How about you take a nap?"

"But Caleb—"

"I'll babysit."

"I don't know . . ."

"You've got nothing to worry about. The kid is fast asleep. You should take a page from his book. Really leads by example, doesn't he?"

I chuckle, the idea of snuggling into my bed for a quick snooze sounding more and more appealing by the second. "A quick nap. If I'm not up in twenty minutes, come get me, okay?"

Saint pretends to contemplate this before ultimately shrugging. "Nah. I'm not gonna do that."

"Saint," I whine. "Please? I don't want to miss anything."

He steers me toward the hallway, giving me the gentlest of pushes toward my room. "And you won't. You deserve to rest, Kinley."

I give Caleb one last longing look before accepting defeat. Saint and my exhaustion win this time around. Next time, it won't be so easy.

"Fine," I grumble, a little annoyed by his insistence, but mostly grateful for it.

The walk down the hall is a blur. I don't remember turning off the lights or crawling under my duvet. I don't even remember what I dream about.

• • •

When I wake up, I feel like a brand-new person. A brand-new person with really swollen boobs. And based on the sound of Caleb crying from the other side of the condo, it's time to feed him.

"Is the pizza here yet?" I ask as I shuffle into the living room, my voice a little froggy from my nap.

Saint is cradling the tiny shape of my son in his arms, whispering words of comfort with that deep, velvety voice of his. When he lifts his gaze to mine, I don't think he's ever been more gorgeous than he is right now, holding my child so gently in his burly arms.

"Welcome back to the land of the living," Saint says, that signature smirk giving me goose bumps. "Pizza arrived about three hours ago."

My jaw just about drops to the floor. I whirl around to look at the clock and find he's right. It's been three hours since I lay down. I must have *really* needed that rest.

"Holy cow." I laugh a little breathlessly. "I'll take him."

Saint slips Caleb into my arms with a smile I feel all the way in my toes, murmuring, "He needs his mama."

I catch myself blushing at his word choice. Turns out I really like it when Saint calls me that.

"He needs *something*." I pull at my maternity top without thinking, undoing the clasp to free one of my breasts. Before I completely expose myself, I look up at Saint. "Um, is this okay?"

His eyes widen and a blush crawls up his neck. He blinks between my eyes and my cleavage, clearly *very* distracted. Maybe this is a bad idea, but I need to feed my kid. Besides, it's kind of fun catching him off guard like this.

"Go ahead. Don't stop on my account. Unless you'd like me to . . ." He gestures toward the door, offering to give me some privacy.

"I'm good if you are."

We settle onto the couch again, sitting in the exact same spots we did in the beginning moments of our first hookup. Caleb is still learning how to latch, so it takes him a while to find my nipple. Saint fusses with the remote control, scrolling through the TV channels and looking at just about anything but me. Maybe this is too much for him after all.

"Am I grossing you out?" I ask through a cringe.

"Not at all," he says, meeting my eyes earnestly. "It's the exact opposite. I'm trying not to stare. You're beautiful, Kinley."

My heart thumps so loudly that I wonder if Caleb can feel it. "Charmer." I giggle, because if I don't laugh, what am I supposed to do? Kiss him?

"I mean it, Kin. Motherhood suits you."

"Thanks, Saint," I murmur. Just hearing that I'm doing a good job makes me feel all warm and gooey inside. "You're not too shabby at the whole caretaker thing either, you know." I shoot him a smile.

"Well . . ." Saint chuckles, leaning back against one of the couch arms. "It's all an act. I'm just trying to impress this girl I like."

My breath catches in my throat. This is it. We're finally having *the conversation*.

"And . . . that's me?" I ask slowly. I need to be

crystal clear on every word if we're going to really talk about it. I don't want to misunderstand or assume.

Saint looks around. "Are there any other beautiful women here?"

"Maybe not, but there are plenty of beautiful women who aren't single mothers."

"And the moment you're ready to not be single anymore, I'll be here."

My heart gives an excited thump. Who knew a professional hockey player could be so frigging adorable?

"Saint . . . thank you. But I don't want a pity partner. You can literally have any woman you want."

"I know. And I'm looking right at her."

All arguments die on my lips, replaced with an irresistible smile. God, he really is a charmer. Hearing him say this is not only flattering, it's affirming. I finally know for a fact that I'm not alone in wanting more. I've tried to push him away, but he never really went far, did he?

Saint runs his hand across the cushion between us to squeeze my knee. It's so natural, so very normal, and somehow exciting at the same time. I can feel the energy between us shifting.

"When I'm ready, you'll be the first to know."

"You know where to find me."

Caleb chooses this precise moment to release my breast with a loud sucking noise and then a wet burp.

Saint smiles at us. "That good, buddy?"

He chuckles, watching me shift Caleb. I laugh as I latch up my nursing bra.

"He's a lucky guy," Saint murmurs, watching us both with a look of admiration that I feel way down in my soul.

18

SAINT

I must have a death wish.

That's the only possible explanation for why I'm currently standing at Reeves's kitchen island of my own volition, waiting as he fills a glass of water for me. I try not to count the number of escape routes in case things get hairy.

I wanted to come here, dammit. I have to do what I came here to do.

I finally told Kinley how I feel. It wasn't dramatic. There weren't any fireworks or choreographed dance mobs. We didn't even kiss because she was nursing the baby at the time. It just happened, like everything else we do. We just happen. We can't seem to stop it, even if there are a bunch of reasons that should be standing in our way.

The brother-shaped obstacle blocking this next step in our relationship is standing right in front of me, sliding a glass of water across the island with a classically sour expression on his face. "You wanted to talk?"

"Yeah, man. Thanks for letting me drop by." I haven't been this nervous since my first NHL game. My heart thumps loudly, but I maintain my composure.

Reeves crosses his arms, narrowing his eyes at me as he waits for me to say what I've come to say.

If I've resolved to jump off a cliff tonight, I might as well do it headfirst. Deal with the consequences later.

"Look, Reeves. I know you don't like me. Hell, I don't even like me sometimes. I'm reckless, and I can be a pain in the ass. I understand that. But I don't want the fact that you don't like me to mess up what I've got going with Kinley. Because whether you like it or not, I'm in love with your sister."

Reeves is a stone wall. We stand there in silence while several seconds tick past.

My agitation grows. *Fuck, is he even hearing me? Am I getting through that thick skull at all?*

"I love Kinley," I say again. "Helping her these past couple of months has changed me. Honestly, I think she helped me more than I ever helped her. I want to be there for her. I want to take care of Caleb. I want to be that guy. And I can't be that guy if you hate my guts. So . . . whatever this shit is between us, can we just get the fuck over it?"

Not the smoothest landing, I'll admit.

But the stony expression on Reeves's face cracks ever so slightly as he sighs, placing both hands on the island and leaning in. I'm not sure if I'm gonna get a heartfelt apology or a death threat. Either way, my heart is in my goddamn throat, and I barely breathe for the next few seconds.

"You're irresponsible."

"I'm responsible enough to keep a job."

"Barely. You're a player."

"Of hockey? A damn good one. And I don't fuck around anymore."

He lifts one eyebrow at me.

Dude, if he only knew. I haven't fucked anyone in . . . I can't even remember. The only girl who gets me hard anymore is his sister, but I doubt he wants to hear that, so I stay quiet.

"You don't care about anyone but yourself."

"That's where you're wrong, Reeves. I care about your sister. A lot. I wouldn't be here if I didn't."

A muscle in his jaw jumps, but for once he doesn't argue with me. Finally, after glaring me down for about as long as I can take without rolling my eyes, he mutters, "Fine."

"Fine?"

"Fine. But if you hurt her—"

"I won't."

"But if you do," he says firmly, delivering the verdict like a judge with anger management issues, "I will literally end you. Do you understand?"

"I won't hurt her."

"Saint. Do you understand me?"

God, this guy is such a drill sergeant. Does he want me to salute?

"Yes. I understand."

"Good."

He reaches out, offering what I think is the first handshake we've shared since we met. I accept it, expecting a death grip. Instead, what I get is firm but painless.

I feel the understanding rooting itself between us. He's just looking out for his little sister. He cares about her as much, or even more than I do. They have a history she and I never will. He doesn't want to see her hurt.

Good thing that's the last thing I'd ever do to Kinley.

"Well, I won't keep you. Thanks for the water." I empty the glass in a few gulps, regaining all the fluids I just lost via nervous sweats. "I'll see ya."

Reeves leads me to the door, patting my back in an oddly familial way before latching it behind me without a word.

I get a pat on the back but no good-bye? I guess I'll have to get used to him now that I'm inserting myself into the Reeves family dynamic. Even if he is an awkward, stick-up-his-ass fuck-wad some-times.

Kinley's place is just down the hall from Reeves's, so I knock softly on the door before let-ting myself in. She's roaming around the living room, the baby tucked against her chest in deep sleep. Classic. He's a marathon napper.

"Hey, you," she says softly, her voice quiet so the baby doesn't stir.

"Hey, gorgeous," I say, keeping my own voice low.

"He just fell asleep. What have you been up to?"

"Oh, just confronting your brother."

Her eyes go comically wide. "You did *what*?"

"I told Reeves that I want a shot with you. And that if he has a problem with that, he can fucking deal with it."

Kinley gasps, catching herself and lowering her voice to a whisper. "You did not."

"I did."

"How did he take it?"

"Oh, as you could expect. Begrudgingly, with plenty of insults peppered in."

"I can't believe you did that."

I nod.

Kinley turns to face me, her expression soft and contemplative. "So, you really want a shot with me?"

"Of course I do."

She waves her hand around her messy living room. "Can you handle all this?"

I think she knows I can. I set up the whole nursery, hosted a baby shower, and stood by her hospital bed while she gave birth. But rather than answer her question, I show her—by gathering her in my arms and giving her a long, slow kiss.

I told her I'd be here whenever she was ready. Do I hope that moment is right now? Yes. But if it's not, I'm prepared to wait.

Kinley is it for me. She's the only woman who's made me want to stick around. Everything is better with her. I'm not going anywhere. As long as it takes.

She gazes up at me with a sweet expression. "I can't believe you talked to my brother."

"If it were just me, I wouldn't care what he thinks. The guy's always hated me, probably always will. But I know that you care about what he thinks. And because you care, I care."

Kinley visibly melts. "Thank you for doing that. I know it couldn't have been easy."

I tuck a strand of hair behind her ear where it came loose from her low ponytail. "It wasn't, but it was worth it. I want you, Kin. And if he's part of the package, well, I can take a few jabs from him every now and then."

"I won't let him bully you. I promise."

I chuckle, leaning over Caleb to kiss her on the forehead and cup her cheeks in my hands. "You have nothing to worry about. I'm in this, one hundred percent."

"Me too."

I cock my head to the side, asking the unspoken question: *Are you sure?*

"I'm ready," she says breathlessly, her gaze locked on my lips.

I comb my fingers through her hair, her ponytail falling out in a smooth cascade. Closing the space between us, I brush my lips against her cheek and her jawline, enjoying how her breathing stutters right before I press my mouth against her plush, eager lips. She opens up to me immediately, tasting sweet like the honey she puts in her chamomile tea.

When our tongues touch, we both groan, deepening the kiss with every stroke and caress. My dick twitches in my jeans when she drags her fingernails against the back of my neck, pulling me as close to her as she can without crushing the baby between us.

Speaking of Caleb and based on the squirming, our tiny third wheel is now wide awake. We part with a laugh, returning our attention to the man of the hour—a very stinky man of the hour.

Kinley giggles. "Wow, he needs a change."

"Talk about a mood killer."

"This is my life. Are you sure you're ready for this?"

"More than ready. I've got him," I say, dropping a kiss onto her forehead and maneuvering his tiny body into my arms. "I'll change his diaper, and then we're going to get right back to that kiss. Stay right here. Do *not* move."

Kinley bursts into laughter. God, I could live off of her smile and nothing else. "Yes, sir. Hurry."

Caleb blinks up at me, and I grin down at him and say, "You heard the lady. Let's do this."

In his nursery, I get to work stripping Caleb down to see what I'm dealing with, and *hoo-ee*, it's *a lot*.

"Dang, that's just impressive," I murmur under my breath.

If you'd have asked me six months ago what

I thought of domestic life, I probably would have run in the opposite direction. Now, there's nowhere else I'd rather be. Stinky diapers and all.

I guess I've just experienced the sweeter side of life now. My days are so much fuller and more meaningful with these two in it.

After I get the little man cleaned up, which included an impromptu bath, he's already half-asleep again. I lay him down in his crib and tiptoe out of the room, careful not to wake him.

This feels like it could be a big moment for Kinley and me. Aside from some early fooling around when she was pregnant, we've never pulled off the hat trick, so to speak.

I find Kinley in her bedroom. The lights are off, and she's sitting on the edge of the mattress. I join her.

"He fell back asleep."

She gives me a grateful look. "Did I hear the water running?"

I nod. "He needed a bath. And a new outfit, but he's clean as a whistle now."

Her eyebrows rise. "You gave him a bath?"

"Of course. I couldn't leave our little man hanging." I mean, he had shit all the way up his back.

Kinley touches my jaw, rubbing her palm over the stubble on my cheek. "You are amazing."

I bring my lips to hers. "So are you."

Sitting on the edge of the bed, we kiss like teenagers until I can't take it anymore. I lie back and move her on top of me, gripping her hips while we kiss. She moves over me, slowly rubbing her sexy curves over my body.

"Can I take this off?" I gesture to her top, and she nods.

"And these?" I rub my hands along her jean-clad thighs.

She hesitates, but then nods again. My heart takes off in a gallop.

I work on stripping her, kissing each new inch of skin I expose. Her soft, breathy sighs are the sweetest sound.

Her eyes meet mine. "I can't, um . . ."

"Have sex?" I fill in the blank rather bluntly, and her lips tip up in a smile.

"Not yet. Not for another few weeks."

That sucks. My body feels like it's going to explode, but I've waited this long. What's a few more weeks? I'd wait forever for Kinley if I had to.

"It's okay," I say. "I'm sorry, I didn't mean to be insensitive . . ."

The rest of that sentence dies on my lips because Kinley is unbuttoning my jeans and pushing her hand inside. I follow her lead, bringing my hand between her thighs and caressing her softly as she moans against my lips.

My body is primed for release, but I ignore the screaming protest of my muscles, the ache in my rigid cock. Tonight is about showing her how much I desire her. How much I appreciate her. How beautiful she is. How desperate she makes me. I need her to come more than I need to breathe.

A few minutes later, she comes apart, gasping and shaking beneath me. I follow her over the edge.

Afterward, we lie together panting, and it's the happiest I've been in a long time.

19

SAINT

They say time flies when you're having fun, but I never gave that saying much thought until recently. I swear, it feels like I blinked for two damn seconds, and before I knew it, two months had flown by.

Don't get me wrong—I was present for every moment of it, long days and even longer nights. Caleb is one hell of a taskmaster for someone who can't even speak yet. When we're not running around at his beck and call, we're barely conscious. The dude sets a rigid schedule.

Sometimes, when Kinley's had an extra-long day, she'll snore right through the crackling noise of the baby monitor. In those moments, I don't mind pulling a little extra weight. It's easy to cover for your fellow coworker when you're in love with her.

Speaking of love, uh, holy shit.

Kinley is unlike any other woman I've ever been with. She's kind and compassionate, somehow managing to call me on my shit while making me laugh the whole while. To think there was a time in my life when I didn't know her . . . A painful ache seizes my chest. That guy was a little lost, a little out of control. Part of me wonders what would have become of him.

But the other part? Well, I don't like to think about that. I prefer to focus on this new life we're creating together.

While we're in talks about moving in together, having separate places does have its perks. Tonight, for instance, will be our first date night out of the complex in months. With Reeves watching the little guy, we'll have time to chill at my place after dinner.

Time I plan to spend worshipping every inch of Kinley's body—if she'll have me.

"If he won't take the bottle, just give me a call and we'll come back," Kinley says as she passes the baby off to Reeves.

He gives us a classically stern look as if to say,

I've got this, okay?

Kinley raises her hands in defeat and tosses her hair over her shoulder. She looks stunning, by the way, in a little black dress that accentuates all her curves like it was tailored specifically for her body.

Fuck, Reeves is right here. I've gotta stop staring at her ass.

"You two deserve a break," Reeves tells her, and I shoot him a grateful glance. "I can stay the night if that would help."

This man is a damn hero. "Actually, that's—"

"Totally not necessary," Kinley cuts in, shaking her head vehemently. "I'm gonna have to feed him again later anyway, so unless you have boobs, I'll need to be here. Actually, it's better if we just come right back after dinner."

All right, so maybe getting Kinley to relax will be more difficult than I originally thought. I guess when you're someone's food source, you can't just take the night off. Even if your boyfriend is desperate to get you naked.

"Thanks again," I call over my shoulder, guiding a very reluctant mother out the door as Reeves waves good-bye with one of Caleb's tiny, yet surprisingly chubby hands.

"Are you sure this is a good idea?" she asks, her hand looping into mine and holding me back before I lead us too far down the hall.

"I actually think this is the best idea we've ever had. C'mon. It'll be okay."

I flash her the slanted grin that always makes her roll her eyes and giggle in equal measure. I've found that it's easier to convince her of something when I use the traits that God gave me. It's a winning smile, what can I say?

"All right. Where are we going?"

"Where do you think?"

Kinley gasps. "Is it the Thai place I like?"

I laugh in disbelief as we enter the parking garage. "We get Thai pretty much every other day. You really think I would take you to the same old place on our first *real* date?"

She blinks, an amused smile stretching across her painted lips. "Oh my God, I guess this kind of is our first date, isn't it?"

"Exactly. I'm treating you. And there's nothing you can do about it."

She raises her hands in gleeful surrender, hopping into the passenger seat when I open the door for her.

It's a quick drive from the complex to the waterside restaurant I've picked out for this special occasion. It's situated on the channel, close enough to the water that the lights are reflected on its rippling surface. We're seated right away, and the first thing Kinley does is peruse the extensive wine list.

"Be honest with me. Is it bad if I order a white right now and then order a red for later?" she asks, chewing on her lower lip with the intensity of an archeologist reading an ancient document.

"It's recommended," I say, flagging the waiter down.

They're very generous with their pours, so we're both already a little tipsy by the time our shared platter of oysters arrives.

"Maybe we should take Reeves up on his offer to stay the night after all," Kinley murmurs over the rim of her wineglass.

I feel her foot trace the line of my calf, pressing intimately against the smooth fabric of my dress pants. Wow, yup, I'm already getting hard. Which is . . . *so* not helpful.

"What makes you say that?" I ask, playing dumb.

Kinley smirks at me and gives me a soft look that I feel right in my groin.

Who knew watching a girl slurp down oysters would be such a turn-on? By the time our entrees arrive, I feel like I'm crawling out of my skin.

All of Kinley's attention immediately turns to the glorious arrangement in front of her: broiled duck, arugula citrus salad, and roasted scallops. The moans that escape her lips as soon as her tongue makes contact with each savory flavor are downright erotic.

Lord help me.

On the way back to the car, she clings to my arm, giggling the whole way. Once we're buckled up, she releases a heavy, reluctant sigh.

"What's wrong?"

"I'm not ready to go back yet."

Hot damn. Here's my opening. "We don't have to go back yet."

Kinley perks up a bit, turning to me and leaning on one arm so her cleavage deepens. "Where would we go? Hey, eyes up here, mister."

I tear my gaze away from her chest with a sheepish smile. "How about we go back to my place?"

"Yeah?" She catches her bottom lip between her teeth, looking me up and down. "Do you think that's a good idea?"

I grin at her. "I think that's the best idea I've ever had."

God, I love her like this—a little tipsy, a little giddy, and a whole lot more relaxed.

As soon as the door to my condo closes behind us, I've got her pushed up against the wall of my entryway.

Kinley whimpers into my kisses, rubbing up against me like a cat in heat. I drop my hands from her hair and down to her round ass, lifting her easily. She wraps her strong legs around my hips like a vise, and I damn near purr with pleasure at the newfound pressure against my straining cock.

Dragging my lips down her neck, I play with the buttons in the front of her little black dress, releasing them one by one until I've got an eyeful of flushed skin against lacy black lingerie.

"Bed?" Kinley asks, breathless.

"Yeah."

I carry her down the hall, stopping once or twice

to crowd her against the wall, against the door—to remind her exactly how badly I want her. I need her to feel how she makes *me* feel. And with the way she grinds her warm center against my raging hard-on, I have no doubt that she wants me just as badly.

We tumble onto the bed in a mess of limbs, tangling up in each other. There's nothing graceful about it. We've waited too long for this moment.

Kinley yanks at my button-down, my belt, the elastic band of my briefs. I occupy myself freeing her gorgeous, plump breasts from her lacy bra, dipping my tongue between the silky mounds to taste her skin. She bucks against me as I pull one taut nipple into my mouth, sucking and swirling.

"Saint . . . kiss me."

Happily.

I trail my kisses back up to her lips, savoring the faint flavor of wine on them. Her warm fingers slide down the front of my pants, pulling me free. I groan at the sensation of her tight fist stroking me, even better than how I remember.

"Whoa there, sweetheart," I murmur, placing one of my hands over hers.

She smiles at me sweetly before gazing down at my obscenely swollen cock in her small hand.

"Feel good?" she asks, her voice filled with desire as she works her hand up and down my length.

I groan. "So good."

When she lowers herself to the floor at my feet, my heart rate accelerates. This isn't what I expected. And when Kinley closes her mouth on my waiting cock, my lungs stop working. Her mouth is hot and eager, and I almost die of happiness on the spot.

Watching Kinley suck and lick me is the most erotic sight. Her fist slides up and down, and her breasts jiggle as she moves over me. She's perfect. I still can't believe she's mine.

"*Fuck*," I breathe out on a moan.

A few minutes more, and I'm closer to the edge than I'd like. Kinley is *really* good at this. I guide her back up and place her in the center of my bed. Once we're both stripped of our remaining clothing, I join her.

"I want you," she murmurs against my lips, nipping at them with her teeth.

My hunger deepens more than I thought possible, like my attraction for Kinley had a false bottom all along and I just discovered a brand-new level of desire.

She kisses me hard on the mouth, wrapping her legs around my hips and pulling me toward her. I can feel the heat radiating from her core—she's ready for me. And God knows I've been ready for a long, long time.

The condom from my bedside table slips onto my throbbing dick with a little help from Kinley's deft fingers. We lie side by side, her eyes on mine. As her palm rests flat against my abs, I touch her everywhere I can—her flushed neck, her breasts, between her thighs.

She groans as my fingers move over her. "Saint . . ." Her voice is filled with need.

I take myself in hand and guide my cock to her center. When she moans and lifts her pelvis, I press in—just a couple of inches. She's so warm and soft around me, I can't believe this is our first time. We've shared so much already, but never *this*. And I'm overcome by the weight of that.

Kinley reaches up to stroke my jaw and tilts my mouth to hers. I press a soft kiss to her lips, and even though I tell myself to go slow in case she needs a minute, my hips move, pressing forward. I sink in a little deeper. It's heaven.

"Feel okay?" My voice comes out deep and rumbly.

"It's perfect," she says breathlessly.

And it really is.

Inch by inch, I fill her, watching the ecstasy bloom on her face with each stretch of new territory. I test my limits by rocking my hips in a gentle rhythm, and she curls around me like a silk ribbon. I don't piston my hips or thrust wildly, I give her time to get where I'm taking her. But trust me, it feels so fucking good that I have a hard time maintaining my slow, steady rhythm. I press my stubbled jaw against the side of her neck and release a slow shaky breath, which may or may not sound like a growl.

"More, yes." She moans, thrusting her hips against me.

Thank God. And who am I to deny her when she asks so nicely?

"Anything for you." I breath out the words.

Our hips move together in perfect time, finding an energetic pace that suits us both. She feels amazing, so warm and wet and perfect.

My thumb finds her clit, and her hips stutter against mine. She loses control as she comes, throwing her head back against the pillows in pleasure. I feel the edge hurtling toward me, so I bury my face in the crook of her neck and hold on to her as I groan through my own powerful release.

When the electric surge of my body finally subsides, I regain awareness of Kinley's body, which is moving against mine. She's *laughing*.

"What are you laughing at?" I mumble, my voice muffled by the sheets.

"Nothing. I'm just happy."

I press a stupid and satisfied grin against her neck. "Me too."

After I muster up the strength to dispose of the condom, we find a prime cuddling position. It takes a little maneuvering of limbs, but once we find it, I never want to move again. I tell her so and she giggles, nipping my arm playfully.

"Sooner or later I'm going to need to go back, you know."

"No . . ." I groan. "Not allowed."

"Well, Walker doesn't have boobs, so his baby-sitting powers are limited."

I shudder at the mental image of Reeves with a rack. "Fair enough."

"Come with me and spend the night?" she asks.

"Of course. Five more minutes?"

She presses a kiss to my cheekbone and nuzzles her nose against mine. "Five more minutes."

20

KINLEY

In the morning, Saint wakes me with a mug of hot coffee in one hand and an alert baby in the other.

"Morning," I murmur, sitting up in bed to take in the sight of them. Caleb is freshly diapered and dressed in the soft gray onesie that I love. And Saint is always a feast for the eyes. They make quite a pair.

"Morning." Saint grins. "Which do you want first?" He makes a point of looking down at each offering—the baby and the coffee, and I laugh. It's a toss up. I *really* love coffee. Even though I only allow myself a few sips of it these days.

"Give me the baby," I say around a yawn, making a grabby hands motion for him.

Saint does with a chuckle, nestling an eager Caleb in beside me on a pillow. I unlatch my top and bring Caleb to my breast while Saint hands me the mug of coffee.

"I had fun with you last night," he says, in that sexy deep voice of his, leaning down to give me a kiss on my cheek.

"Me too," I say, skin heating at the memory of our first-time making love. I knew it would be good, I just didn't know it would be *that* good. Saint was a beast—focused solely on my pleasure. And *woo*, was it pleasurable.

Part of me can't believe this is my life—that I have a sweet, attentive *sex-god* for a boyfriend, and an adorable baby who I love with my whole heart. I definitely didn't see all this coming when I got dumped last year. I'm happier than I have any right to be. I can't even complain about the lack of sleep because so far Caleb is cooperating like a champ. I give him a tender kiss on his chubby cheek.

With another appreciative look, Saint heads to the closet and begins undressing.

"Did you go for a run?" I ask, helping myself to a sip of coffee.

"Yeah," he calls back. "Caleb likes the running stroller, so it worked out well. I went about three miles, I didn't want to push my luck."

Saint had been wanting to begin taking Caleb on his morning jog, but I was nervous with him being so little that his head would flop around. We'd been waiting until Caleb was a little older. I can't believe how quickly my baby is growing. I lean over him and press a gentle kiss to his forehead. He blinks up at me drowsily.

"He should nap for you now. All that fresh air, I'm guessing."

I nod and set the coffee mug aside, then stroke Caleb's fine hair. "Are you heading out?"

"Just for an hour or so. There's a team weight training session this morning with a new trainer. I figured I better not miss it." Saint reappears beside the bed and touches my shoulder. "You look beautiful like this, by the way," he says, gazing down at me.

I still don't know what I did to deserve this man. My throat gets tight with emotion. I'm sitting in a disheveled bed with messy hair and a baby latched to my boob. Meanwhile, my boyfriend who is a literal pro-athlete looks like he could be in a Nike commercial with his athletic wear and muscled physique.

"Maybe when you get home we could..." I gaze

up at him, hoping he'll read between the lines and save me the embarrassment of propositioning him for sex while I'm nursing.

He grins. "I already texted your brother."

My brain screeches to a halt. Does Saint think we need a babysitter every time we want to have sex? I'm about to set him straight and explain that Caleb naps *a lot* when Saint begins talking again.

"I'm taking you for a pedicure."

Just like one of our first dates…

"And maybe to get ice cream?"

My mouth lifts in a smile. He remembers. That day was perfect. It was the day I started falling for Saint, even though I didn't have any right to.

His voice lowers. "And then back to my place."

My heart rate kicks up.

He adjusts himself by sticking his hand into the front of his shorts. "*Fuck*. I'm getting hard just thinking about last night."

I chuckle. I really do love this man.

"Later," I promise.

"Later," he agrees.

Later finally arrives.

My brother is about thirty minutes late and then the pedicures take forever. We abandon the idea of ice cream altogether. All I want in the world is to be alone with Saint, even if it is pretty awesome to have my neglected feet tended to.

When we reach Saint's place, he unlocks the door and then we're kissing, right there in the foyer.

"Thank you for today," he says, but it comes out jumbled because I can't stop kissing his perfect mouth. He chuckles against my lips. I make an inarticulate sound.

"You in a rush all of a sudden?" His mouth lifts in a crooked smile.

"Tell me you haven't been thinking about this all day."

He sinks his teeth into his lip.

"That's what I thought."

He touches my neck and urges my mouth to his. He keeps one hand there, his thumb lightly stroking the rapid pulse in my neck while the other cups my breast. He pinches my nipple and I feel my knees tremble.

Somehow, I've unbuttoned his jeans and I push my hands into his briefs, drawing them down his thighs. I'm practically shaking with need and I can feel Saint almost vibrating with anticipation too. You would think last night would have taken the edge off our lust for each other, but somehow it had the opposite effect. When I wrap him in my fist, he makes a breathless noise. He's alarmingly hard for me. And of course I freaking love it.

His hands are everywhere, massaging my ass, cupping the generous swells of my breasts, tilting my mouth up to his… It's like he can't get enough of me. I feel the exact same way. I want every part of him and I want it *right now*. He pushes my leggings down my legs and I pull my top off over my head, dropping it on the floor beside us.

His kisses are urgent and hot, and oh, *wow*, I need him. Abandoning the foreplay, I climb into his lap as he sinks down onto the couch.

"Baby, wait." His voice is rough, barely above a growl.

Wait? The word wait doesn't resonate. It has no meaning. I can't wait. Not even to move this party into his bedroom. Saint seems to understand. The need between us is too great.

He shifts my panties to the side and when he feels how ready I am for him, he groans.

"*Fuck*, Kinley."

He uses the slickness to press his fingers inside and then sweeps them over my clit. He keeps right on kissing me while I whimper and moan and writhe above him. I feel dizzy with desire.

I grip his biceps to keep my balance and begin lowering myself down. Saint brings one hand between us to position himself at the right angle, and then I'm being stretched around him. Saint's hands at my waist lift and lower me, and just like last night, he doesn't pound or pummel into me. His rhythm is maddeningly slow and steady, allowing everything to build. And build, it does.

I feel so full of him and so loved. He kisses me through it all, telling me how much he loves me, and how good I feel. His lips move to my neck and I rock against him, desperate to move faster, to have more of him.

Saint suddenly shifts and I realize I'm being lifted—being placed on my back on the sofa, and then he's moving over top of me, joining us again. I arch my back and welcome the intrusion. The feeling of fullness is perfect, and when he brings his thumb to my clit, I let out a very loud, very eager sound.

"Yes," I say, panting.

"You are so perfect," he groans, his eyes moving over me—from the spot where he's still moving deliberately to my heavy breasts that wobble on each smooth thrust.

His thumb does wonderful things and I find myself racing toward my release faster than I thought possible.

"Saint!" I groan, my fingers fighting for purchase on his muscled thighs.

It's then that his measured strokes finally falter. He begins moving faster, harder, and with each thrust, he hits just the right spot. My eyes sink closed and I can't hold out any longer. Pleasure spirals through me, greater than I've ever known. I come apart with a strangled cry, his name leaving my lips over and over again while Saint continues to pound into me, his own low moans now joining mine.

"Baby, fuck." I feel a spasm move through him and he makes the sexiest sound, burying his face into my neck. He doesn't move his body from mine, but he begins kissing me all over—my forehead, neck and collarbone, and it is perfect. Watching him lose control just became my favorite new pastime.

EPILOGUE

KINLEY

One year later

The second baby shower of my life is a little less stressful than the first.

For starters, Aspen offered to help with the planning and setup, taking some of the weight off of Saint's shoulders this time around. Once all of our moving boxes were unpacked and the new house was in good enough shape for visitors, Aspen organized everything for us—light refreshments, a couple of non-humiliating baby-themed games, and even a gift registry for the brand-new little one.

Secondly, I actually know the guests this time around. Everyone who was invited last time is invited again this time. When they arrive, Saint and I take turns greeting each one, exchanging hugs and inside jokes. Having spent the last year getting to know the team and their wives, I feel like they're a big extended family.

Caleb toddles by us, squealing with excitement as Saint follows after him, making scary pirate noises that have my fourteen-month-old dissolving into a fit of giggles. Pirate Chase is their favorite game, and Saint is always devoted to giving Caleb his complete and undivided attention whenever they play.

It's adorable. I don't think I'll ever tire of watching them play.

"Coming through."

Eden's crystalline voice cuts through the noise as she and Holt waltz into the foyer. She has multiple gift bags hanging from her arms, and her husband is carrying a box so big that it nearly doesn't fit through the doorway.

"Eden, welcome," I say, returning a kiss on the cheek.

"So sorry we're late, Kinley. We hit traffic on the way here. I found so many lovely things for you. I left all the receipts in the bags in case you want to return anything." She lifts her arms, showing off the gift bags. "More comfy-cozy clothes for my favorite mama, and that"—she points to the box Holt is tucking under the gift table—"is a Snoo. Have you ever heard of a Snoo? It's very highly rated on all the luxury motherhood forums."

"Oh God, Eden. Aren't those really expensive?"

She shrugs. "There's no price tag on the future of our children. Enjoy." With that, she loops her arm in Holt's and wanders through the house, giving herself the grand tour.

I can't keep up with this woman, but damn, do I admire her energy. And Holt's, for that matter. Not every man could keep up with a force like Eden Wynn.

Summer passes by with two beers in hand, giving one to Logan with a soft kiss on his cheek. They got married two years ago, and it couldn't be any clearer that they're head over heels for each other. So in love, in fact, that I'm going to have to keep an eye on them and make sure they don't start canoodling in front of my kiddo.

Freaking lovebirds.

Speaking of my best guy, Caleb is tuckered out after running laps around Saint, who easily lifts him into his arms. Caleb immediately lays his head on Saint's broad shoulder as Saint follows Alex out onto the deck, laughing from somewhere deep in his chest.

I peer after Saint, sneaking a peek at his ass in those jeans I like so much.

God, my man is so effortlessly sexy. I'd say it was unfair if I didn't get to reap all the benefits. He catches me staring and shoots me a wink that has me blushing up to my hairline.

Lord. Maybe we're the lovebirds here.

After Walker arrives, he drops off a small box on the gift table.

I swear to God, if those are car keys, I'm gonna punch him. The man is determined to get me a new model every year, always claiming that the safety improves with each update. As soon as I get used to a new car, I have to learn how to drive a whole new model. And yes, I know—this is *the* first-world problem of all first-world problems.

Before I can sneak a peek inside the box, Aspen catches my hand.

"All right, everyone's here," she says. "This is going to be so fun."

My heart swells with gratitude. "Thank you so much for setting all this up, Aspen."

"It's my pleasure."

Just then, I feel a tug on my skirt.

"Mama?"

I look down to see Caleb gazing up at me with his big brown eyes.

He's still a shy talker, only using around five or six words regularly, but I'd recognize that expression anywhere. My little guy is bored now that Saint is busy chatting with his friends. Caleb needs a playmate.

"I've got this." Aspen kneels down to Caleb's level. "Wanna show me your cool art projects over there?"

Caleb pulls Aspen's hand, dragging her over to his craft corner, where all his creations have been meticulously taped to the wall by yours truly. I catch Alex staring after the two of them, a soft expression on his face.

Interesting. Maybe Camille and I won't be the only moms in the group for much longer.

Later that night, when we've all gathered together on the deck, I raise my glass of nonalcoholic seltzer water to make a toast to my friends.

"Thank you all for coming tonight. It feels like just yesterday that you all attended my first baby shower. I'm so grateful to each of you for making room for me in your lives and truly accepting me as one of your own. I'm already looking forward to the next one."

"The next one?" Logan gapes comically, dodging a playful smack from Summer.

Saint wraps his arm around my shoulders and takes over. "I don't know about Kin, but I'm building a small army. Isn't that right, Caleb?"

"Uh-huh." Caleb cheers, inspiring hoots and hollers all around us.

"Whoa, there," Alex says, cutting in with a wry grin. "Slow down, crazies. Holy baby factory."

"To the baby factory," Aspen says cheerfully, raising her glass high.

Cheers ricochet from person to person, and laughter all around. Even Caleb joins in, his infectious little giggle adding to the joy.

Saint pulls me in close, pressing a kiss to my temple. I can feel the pride he has for our family radiating from his touch. I lean into his embrace, relishing in this strange and wonderful life we've hodge-podged together with craft glue and diaper adhesives. It isn't perfect, but it's everything to me.

Turns out my life in Boston wasn't so bad after all. Luckily for me, there's so much more adventure yet to come.

· · ·

Later that night, Saint tucks Caleb into his new toddler bed, and I curl up in the center of ours. I'm seven months pregnant now and feeling more tired than I remember with my first pregnancy.

"Hey." Saint grins when he sees me.

"Hey." Sleepily, I smile back. "You think he'll actually stay in there tonight?"

Caleb began climbing out of his crib, and I was worried he'd fall and hurt himself. But the trouble with the toddler bed has been that he's been getting up at weird hours of the night.

"I think so. He crashed right away. I think the party today wore him out."

"He's not the only one," I say around a yawn.

Saint chuckles and heads to the master closet where he begins undressing. My husband's muscles flex as he moves around the room, and I lay quietly, appreciating the view. I don't think I'll ever get tired of just admiring him. His body is a masterpiece that he works hard to maintain. Powerful thighs, an adorable muscular butt, defined abs and shoulders I love to cling to. It's a good thing he likes my body, even in pregnancy.

Dressed in only a pair of gray athletic shorts slung low on his hips, he goes through his regular bedtime routine—checks to make sure all the doors are locked, arms the alarm system, and brings me a glass of water, which he sets on my bedside table before pressing a kiss to my forehead.

Saint and I got married at the courthouse when Caleb was about six months old. We took a short honeymoon in the Bahamas. Well, maybe it was more of a family vacation and less of a honeymoon, because Caleb and my brother came along.

Walker was great about babysitting so that Saint and I could have some alone time. We rented a house for almost two weeks . . . one big happy family.

I'm really thankful that my brother and Saint have worked out their differences. Their struggles to get along now seem so foreign. I know Walker was only looking out for me, and now that he knows how good Saint is to me, there's no animosity left between them.

When Saint finally crawls into bed beside me a few minutes later, he moves closer and gathers me in his arms. "Are you still sleepy?" he asks, running one hand down my spine.

I shift closer and feel that he's hard. Either that,

or there's a baseball bat between us.

"A little," I say, my heart quickening. I am tired, but he's a hard man to resist.

I run one hand down his sculpted chest and let out a happy sigh. My hand comes to a stop at the waistband of his shorts, and then I venture lower, running a palm along the hard length of him. Slowly. Teasingly.

Saint inhales sharply. "Don't, baby. If you're tired, I can wait."

I grin into the darkness. So selfless. This man really is a saint. It makes me want to give him all the things he desires. And based on the way he's kissing my neck and slowly rocking his hips into mine . . . what he desires most is *me*.

"Your brother called earlier, by the way."

"Are we really gonna talk about my brother right now?" I smirk. My hand is on his cock.

"Absolutely not." His voice is serious, but playful.

I slip my hand under the elastic of Saint's shorts and find him commando, not to mention incredibly hard. I tease and stroke him until he's groaning quietly.

"Baby . . . *Fuck*. Feels good."

Silently, I remove my cotton sleep shorts and guide Saint closer. We don't use protection anymore . . . which is why I guess I ended up pregnant a few weeks before our wedding.

Whoops.

But no one was the wiser, and Saint was over the moon to add to our family. He's such an amazing dad, but awesome-dad vibes are the last thing on my mind right now because Saint is moving over me, joining us with a long, slow thrust.

I exhale loudly and grip his muscular backside, urging him to move faster.

"You okay?" He breathes out the words, and I groan.

He's always checking in on me. I love it.

I'm not sure who Saint was before I came into his life, but this man gives me everything I need. A stable, loving home for my son, as well as safety, security, and love. And not to mention the sex is incredible.

"I love you," I murmur, my lips on his.

"Love you more."

• • •

Thank you so much for reading! To find out what I have coming up next, make sure you sign up to receive my emails here:
www.kendallryanbooks.com/newsletter

Get Two Free Books

Sign up for my newsletter and I'll automatically send you two free books.

www.kendallryanbooks.com/newsletter

Follow Kendall

Website

www.kendallryanbooks.com

Facebook

www.facebook.com/kendallryanbooks

Twitter

www.twitter.com/kendallryan1

Instagram

www.instagram.com/kendallryan1

Newsletter

www.kendallryanbooks.com/newsletter

Other Books by Kendall Ryan

Down and Dirty

Crossing the Line

Wild for You

Taking His Shot

How to Date a Younger Man

Penthouse Prince

The Boyfriend Effect

My Brother's Roommate

The Stud Next Door

The Rebel

The Rival

The Rookie

The Rebound

For a complete list of Kendall's books, visit:
www.kendallryanbooks.com/all-books/

Acknowledgments

A humongous bear hug to my editor Pam Bere-hulke. To Alyssa Garcia, thank you for putting up with me. I know I'm forgetful and a little crazy, but I want you to know I appreciate the heck out of you, and I'm so thankful we're on this journey together. Rachel Brookes, your enthusiasm for my stories is always appreciated and I'm grateful for you and your friendship. Thank you to Stacy Garcia for your unending excitement and support of my stories. You always bring a smile to my face. Thank you to Kelly Emery for the beautiful graphics you create and for making my social pages look so pretty. Thank you to Virginia Carey for your eagle-eye.

A heartfelt thank-you to all the readers who have followed this series. I have so enjoyed writing about these tough, yet sweet hockey players and the strong women they fall for. Thank you to the members of my Facebook group and all the bloggers for your support. I heart you!